RELIEF | A QUARTERLY CHRISTIAN EXPRESSION

VOLUME ONE | ISSUE THREE

RELIEF | A QUARTERLY CHRISTIAN EXPRESSION

EDITOR-IN-CHIEF
Kimberly Culbertson

ASSISTANT EDITOR
Heather von Doehren

FICTION EDITOR
J. Mark Bertrand

CREATIVE NONFICTION EDITOR
Karen Miedrich-Luo

POETRY EDITOR
Brad Fruhauff

TECHNICAL EDITOR
Coach Culbertson

EDITORIAL ASSISTANT
Margaret Krueger

COPY EDITORS
Alan Ackmann
Meggan Green
Lisa Ohlen Harris
Margaret Krueger

READERS
Allison Smythe—Poetry
Lisa Ohlen Harris—Creative Nonfiction
Mick Silva—Fiction
Alan Ackmann—Fiction

Relief: A Quarterly Christian Expression is published quarterly by ccPublishing, NFP, a 501(c)3 organization dedicated to advancing Christian literary writing. Mail can be sent to 60 W. Terra Cotta, Suite B, Unit 156, Crystal Lake, IL 60014-3548. Submissions are not accepted by mail.

SUBSCRIPTIONS

Subscriptions are $48 per year and can be purchased directly from the publisher by visiting http://www.reliefjournal.com. Single issues are also available.

COPYRIGHT

All works Copyright 2007 by the individual author credited. Anything not credited is Copyright 2007 by ccPublishing, NFP. No part of this publication may be reproduced, stored in a retrieval system, or transmitted by any means without prior written permission of ccPublishing, NFP.

SUBMISSIONS

Submissions are open year round via our Online Submisison System. Please visit our website at **http://www.reliefjournal.com** for instructions. Sorry, but we are unable to read or return submissions received by mail.

THANK YOU

We thank the following people who, by subscribing before the first issue or by donating, have financially supported *Relief*.

WE OWE EXTRAORDINARY GRATITUDE TO OUR DONORS: HEROES:

HEATHER ACKMANN
THE MASTER'S ARTIST @ HTTP://WWW.THEMASTERSARTIST.COM
ROBERT AND LAURA BAKER

AND TO THE REST OF OUR FOUNDERS, WHO HAVE HELPED US TO MAKE THIS JOURNAL A REALITY:

VASTHI ACOSTA
ADRIENNE ANDERSON
KARI L. BECKEN
JILL BERGKAMP
STEVE BOGNER
SUSAN BOYER
SUSAN H. BRITTON
SHAWN COHEN
JONATHAN D. COON
CHAD COX
JEANNE DAMOFF
DIANNA DENNIS
BEN DOLSON
STEVE ELLIOTT
CHRISTOPHER FISHER
DEEANNE GIST
DEBORAH GYAPONG
SYLVIA HARPER
APRIL HARRISON
MATTHEW HENRY
GINA HOLMES
LEANNA JOHNSON
JILL KANDEL
MICHAEL KEHOE
BILL AND PEGGIE KRUEGER
ALLISON LEAL
DAVID LONG
JEROMY MATKIN

ANDREW MEISENHEIMER
CHRISTOPHER MIKESELL
CHARMAINE MORRIS
MARGARET M. MOSELEY
SARAH NAVARRO
NANCY NORDENSON
KAREN T. NORRELL
RANDY PERKINS
SHANNA PHILIPSON
CALEB ROBERTS
SUZAN ROBERTSON
CHRISTINA ROBERTSON
LISA SAMSON
LANDON SANDY
AOTEAROA EDITORIAL SERVICES
MICHAEL SNYDER
CATHERINE STAHL
DOROTHEE SWANSON
AMBER TILSON
SHERRI TOBIAS
PHIL WADE
DAVID WEBB
CHRISTINA WEEKS
REBEKAH WILKINS-PEPITON
MARYANNE WILIMEK
MANKATO
AND THOSE WHO PREFER TO REMAIN ANONYMOUS

If you would also like to help keep the journal going, please visit our website, www.reliefjournal.com and click on Support The Cause.

TABLE OF CONTENTS

FROM THE EDITOR'S DESK KIMBERLY CULBERTSON	6
COACH'S CORNER COACH CULBERTSON	8

EDITOR'S CHOICE

SINS OF THE FATHERS FICTION BY BY J. BRISBIN	10
SOMETIMES THE PLAGUES ARE SCHEDULED POETRY BY MAUREEN TOLMAN FLANNERY	16
AN OVERTURE'S TURN CREATIVE NONFICTION BY DEANNA HERSHISER	17

FICTION

GOODBEY SOPHIE DON HOESEL—WINNER OF THE FAITH * IN * FICTION DAILY SACRAMENT CONTEST	24
THE MATING HABITS OF LIZARDS ANGIE POOLE—RUNNER-UP OF THE FAITH * IN * FICTION DAILY SACRAMENT CONTEST	34
MISS SWEETY'S ROCK-OLA MACHINE J. MARCUS WEEKLEY	44
JESUS CALLED ELLEN MORRIS PREWITT	64
SAINTS OF COLORADO CHRISTOPHER ESSEX	74
A MIRACLE FOR MARTY LOIS BARLIANT	106

CREATIVE NONFICTION

DANCES WITH OLIVIA ALYS MATTHEWS	51
WE THE PEOPLE OF BARBIE RENEE RONIKA KLUG	53
DILL JILL KANDEL	70
ESTHER: A REMEMBRANCE RICHARD WILE	85
PHOTOGRAPHING THE CROSS CALEE MILAN LEE	98

POETRY

FEAST DAY OF ST. URSULA DEBRA KAUFMAN	47
EASTER DEBRA KAUFMAN	48
APRIL FOOLS DEBRA KAUFMAN	41
GRACE DEBRA KAUFMAN	42
SHE CANNOT REMEMBER SOCRATES S. JASON FRALEY	60
BECAUSE THERE IS NO EASY ANSWER S. JASON FRALEY	61
STANDARD AND DISTINCT THINGS GREGORY O'NEILL	63
BOYS OF IONA PREP ANN CEFOLA	67
ST. AGNES, PINKSLIPPED ANN CEFOLA	68
SECOND WHITSUN MAURENN TOLMAN FLANNERY	72
LETTER TO THE CHURCHES CHRISTOPHER MULROONEY	84
FOR JUDAS ISCARIOT CICELY ANGLETON	90

MOVING LUCY VEGA TO THE RESERVATION PAUL LUIKART	91
ANUNCIATION: TRIPTYCH ANNE M. DOE OVERSTREET	96
IN THIS PLACE OF GRASS ANNE M. DOE OVERSTREET	97
FLOTSAM JEFF P. JONES	102
EL ORACION DE LA CIUDAD HEATHER MICHELLE STEWART	

COVER ART

THIS ISSUE'S COVER, *GREEN GIRLS*, WAS BUILT BY TECHNICAL EDITOR COACH CULBERTSON. ORIGINAL PHOTO, "STARING AT YOUR FEET," BY KATHRYN MCCALLUM.

PLUS!

LOOK FOR A BONUS STORY, "THE DELUGE" BY MATT MIKALATOS, AT THE END OF THE JOURNAL. YOU'LL ENJOY THE PREVIEW OF *COACH'S MIDNIGHT DINER*, THE GENRE ANTHOLOGY COMING IN 2007 FROM CCPUBLISHING.

IN MEMORY OF CHRISTOPHER ESSEX
"SAINTS OF COLORADO"

FEBRUARY 19, 1965–APRIL 17, 2007

FROM THE EDITOR'S DESK KIMBERLY CULBERTSON
EDITOR-IN-CHIEF

THERE WAS A TIME IN MY LIFE when I knew who I was. I was mighty in the strength of that knowledge. I knew who God would have me be, I wanted to be her, and I knew I *was* her, even though I fouled up quite a bit. That confidence lasted, well, about two days. Maybe three.

The lies I have believed about myself have beaten me senseless. I have warred against them to define an identity outside of other people's expectations, to begin to see a person I was built to be. It is only with God's profound influence that fear and insecurity have become less powerful in my every moment.

I'd like to report that after moments of divine inspiration and epiphany I have held onto the resultant wisdom carefully, that what God showed me about me remained paramount, lording its intense reality over all of the mythologies I've faced, that those lies no longer have a vice grip on my self-perception. But it seems I was born with an addiction to image and approval.

Even this strong sense of identity from God has not left me immune. Even as an adult, I still want my dad to be proud of me, still long to be the "best friend," still question what I know God has done in me because the people around me do. I am still shaken when my family and friends are disappointed by my choices, even when I am certain that they are the choices I should have made, and would happily make again—if only my husband and I could exist in a vacuum with God.

Recently, Ben and I struggled with some big life decisions; we knew what we would end up doing, but we were still struggling with fear. We had to admit to ourselves that all of our reservations found their sources in the what-would-so-and-so-think types of fears. I worried about explaining myself to my dad. I worried that my friends would think I was naïve. I worried about being considered a failure, or worse, that if things went badly, others would perceive the failure to be God's. And after some soul searching and prayer, I had to relearn a few things: first, that love and generosity are not made null by the fact that sometimes people fail us, and that what many people might consider a failure, God might consider success; second, that God can handle Himself if people misunderstand or get angry with Him; and finally, that somewhere along the line, I have again let people's perceptions of me trump not only God's perception, but also my own—and while other's expectations have often affected me, protecting their illusions has never brought me fulfillment. So in this moment, I feel peace and strength. Two days and counting.

Judging from this issue's submissions, I am not alone. This issue is filled with work that struggles with identity. Friends and bystanders contemplate those who do not fit the mold, finding beauty in a goth dancer, a welfare mother cultivating chaos in suburbia, a gangly young man on a sugar high, a child with a priestly calling. Characters struggle with history, both personal and generational, from slavery to incarceration, and feel the weight of it as they craft their own identities or try to achieve a new beginning. Outside forces, from poverty to corporate America to Barbie threaten to redefine and judge the characters, the church, even the identity of a hospital. Authors in this issue have asked tough questions about what really makes something beautiful, valuable, successful, and spiritual.

In each issue, we have chosen to showcase a piece from each genre by honoring the author with the "Editor's Choice Award." In Issue Three, we offer our congratulations to J. Brisbin for his story "Sins of the Fathers," Maureen Tolman Flannery for her poem "Sometimes the Plagues are Scheduled," and Deanna Hershiser for her creative nonfiction piece "An Overture's Turn." Brisbin's story watches generational turmoil through the mind's eye of a prisoner being punished in a hotbox. The title provokes a layered contemplation of generational sin, from the sins of our founding fathers to Jesus's answer of "neither" when he is questioned regarding for whose sin a blind man is being punished. Flannery's poem struggles with the identity of a God who would deliberately harden a person's heart to achieve his goals, and questions the personal identity of a Christian attempting evangelism and an unhearing audience. The poem is exciting from the first word, persuasion, with it's interesting dual meaning; is it the speaker's religious persuasion that hardens the heart of the listener, or does the listener simply revolt against being persuaded? Hershiser's essay follows a Christian woman who steps out of her comfort zone to befriend a woman after others have deemed themselves too good for her. In her journey she redefines beauty and goodness, and when reality does not match her expectations, she finds herself at odds with the cookie cutter answers that are offered to her.

Crucial in the identity of a writer, especially for those who "write for God," is the hope that something in the work will resonate in the audience, affecting the reader long after the book has been shelved. I believe that individuals, especially those who hope for a close connection with Christ, are constantly working to discover how to view themselves and others, and that the work is not likely to be finished this side of heaven. May this issue challenge you if you have become comfortable, may it soothe you if you are lost, and may you enjoy every page.

RELIEF | A QUARTERLY CHRISTIAN EXPRESSION
CONGRATULATES THE WINNERS OF ITS
EDITOR'S CHOICE AWARDS

<u>FICTION</u>
J. BRISBIN
SINS OF THE FATHERS

<u>POETRY</u>
MAUREEN TOLMAN FLANNERY
SOMETIMES THE PLAGUES ARE SCHEDULED

<u>CREATIVE NONFICTION</u>
DEANNA HERSHISER
AN OVERTURE'S TURN

WE ALSO CONGRATULATE THE WINNERS OF THE
FAITH * IN * FICTION DAILY SACRAMENT CONTEST

<u>WINNER</u>
DON HOESEL
GOODBYE SOPHIE

<u>RUNNER-UP</u>
ANGIE POOLE
THE MATING HABITS OF LIZARDS

THE DAILY SACRAMENT CONTEST ASKED WRITERS TO CAPTURE THE EVERYDAY IN LIGHT OF THE ETERNAL AND THE SACRED IN THE SURROUNDINGS OF THE COMMONPLACE. THE CONTEST WAS JUDGED BY J. MARK BERTRAND, FICTION EDITOR OF RELIEF, AND DAVID LONG, AUTHOR OF THE FAITH * IN * FICTION BLOG AT HTTP://WWW.FAITHINFICTION.BLOGSPOT.COM.

SINS OF THE FATHERS J. BRISBIN

OF EPHREM WALLACE LEE JACOBY who came to the New World to escape persecution but found or was found by it anyway and of Meredith Rose Jacoby who harvested shrubs and massaged swollen bellies and remembered her own family's family who were not Good People but wretched and treacherous (bought, it's said, by an aversion to industry or any quality in their personage which would allow them to provide for their own rumbling stomachs) and of the hungry mouths and minds descended in bounty though shackled to a corpse and of Jacob Raymond Lee who bluffed against a pair of eights and forgot to return things borrowed and of manacles and five-nines and rendering flesh and of a place whispered and shouted about but only visited once or never and a home but that over yonder.

COB WAKES UP.

He's sitting down. Oak planks against his back hold him up. It's too dark to see. He flails an arm around, looking for a wall and skins his knuckles on one a foot away. He tries to stretch his legs and his chained feet rattle—a door? Shackles jangle on his wrists as he raises numb fingers to his quaking face. He's never been in the hot-box before, so he doesn't recognize the stench and the calloused oak of wall and floor.

"When a man's hands get calloused, they crack and roughen," Cob's grandpa Lee had said, rubbing sore hands together gently, "but oak gets smooth and becomes gentle." His red hands floated down to the arms of the rocking chair and stroked them gently.

Cob touches his cheek and remembers the worn, checker-patterned steel butt plate of a shotgun flying toward his face. The image is a photograph, frozen in time. He can see wood, steel, and gleaming, barred teeth. He knows he can't dodge it. The image unfreezes and he sees sky, then dirt. His head expands and contracts in tempo with his heartbeat. He expects to find sticky blood on his face but feels none. Fingers brush against something stuck to his face that feels like a small piece of thread hanging from a scab.

Great-grandma always had threaded needles stuck in her clothes somewhere. Cob would lean in to give her a hug and she'd push him away: "I'm sewing, Jacob, there's needles here." Grandpa would scold her for it and she'd sigh and give Cob a pat on the top of his head.

Voices float through the horizontal slit in the door Cob can't see but knows is there. He leans forward and tastes a wisp of fresh air that wanders too close. He hears two men arguing. Judging the distance as best he can, he figures them to be near the main barracks hall of the prison, across an open space from the hot-box and outhouses. Pain rushes toward his forehead like water sloshing in a bowl that isn't carried carefully, so he leans back.

LEG IRONS CHINK as a ten-stone slug of steel on the end of a three-and-a-half-foot handle come down with a thump, crack. Limestone sparks and splits open with a puff of dust and a sigh. Sweat drips from Cob's forehead. He wipes it with the sleeve of a faded, striped uniform and turns to find Huddy. His escape is less than a week away and he has to reassure himself. Like the stripes, light and dark prisoners stay in their own lines; dark on the south side of the road, light on the north. Huddy doesn't turn around. A new chorus begins and everyone, light or dark, thump, cracks in time to the story of ancient Hebrews (thump, crack) saved from a Pharaoh and the parting of a sea. Thump, crack and the Israelites free.

The plan demanded Huddy's unnaturally accurate hammer swing. If he struck the leg irons perfectly, they would deform; not enough to notice, but enough to wiggle out an ankle then a heel then a foot. Without the leg irons, Cob could out-smart the dogs, out-run the leeches, and end up on a train bound for Chicago. If Huddy missed, Cob would never walk again.

A sorrel mare trots up and stops in front of Cob. He looks up. The guard's hand goes from reins to rifle. Cob turns around and the guard waits to click his mouth at the horse until he sees the sledge come up and go down. Thump, crack and manna from Heaven; pillar of fire by day and a scourge of snakes and a thump, crack.

The day gets smaller and Cob splits a rock in two and makes two out of each of those two and so on and so forth. Muscles cramp and hands bleed, but instead of rocks, Cob pretends they're leg irons. He swings hard and the guard smiles at his industry and the horse paws the ground. Shadows lay down across the road but the light and dark stripes keep working.

IT'S QUIET OUTSIDE THE HOT-BOX NOW. The men have stopped arguing. Cob hears a door slam and the warden's dog barks. He hears singing coming toward him, too low and gentle to hear words. The voice is close now and stops.

"You awake, Jacob?"

Cob doesn't answer. A light shoots through the slit and scalds his eyes. He jabs his arm at it and the light goes away.

The door rattles a little and there's a slow creak on the step followed by a tired sigh. An orange glow flashes and sweet cigarette smoke trickles into the box.

"I'm sorry about this, Jacob. I wish't didn't have to be this way."

A sustained note, like a plucked string that's allowed to ring until it dissipates its energy, then: "I'm sorry as hell about your face, Jacob."

The darkness at the slit gets darker. "You want a cigarette?"

Although he doesn't smoke, Cob mumbles a thanks and leans forward. Shackles jangle as he feels for the proffered roll. He finds it, puts his lips on the end, and waits for the warden to light it. He sees the orange flash of the match illuminate a shaved cheek glistening with sweat. The light goes away and Cob leans back. He coughs on the sandpapery smoke that goes down into his lungs and refuses to leave. The warden laughs.

"Not much of a smoker if you choke on Turkish tobacco. Damned Ottomans weren't good for much, but they sure knew how to grow tobacco. We ended up with a case of it during the War. Had to clear out a Boche trench to get it, though."

Five-nines started screaming again and Cob thought he felt the hot-box shake. The warden shifted his weight on the step.

"You were in the War, weren't you, Jacob?"

Crickets and locusts redouble their patterned chirping.

"Yes, sir," Cob mumbles.

DEAD SMELL HAD BEEN EVERYWHERE—in the trench, in no-man's, in the hospital, in town. Where there was dead smell, there were dead—in the ground, on the ground, all over the ground. There was one thick-trunked oak tree left between a stretch of Allied and enemy trenches. It was called The Hand. The stubborn trunk held up a tassel of splintered finger-limbs like it was reaching out of the alien geography and grasping at something. One morning, when it was just light enough to see, both trench lines went quiet for a quarter-hour. The Hand grasped a young boy missing one leg and both hands. His ratted uniform flapped gently in a cool breeze. An artillery shell had shredded his uniform, rolled him in barbed wire, and tossed him into the tree. Out of respect, a French lieutenant dropped several rounds of 75s on them and the boy and The Hand went away.

"YOU KNOW, IT'S BETTER FOR YOU AND HUDDY you never got the chance to escape," the Warden says.

Sweet smoke smell and the Warden: "If you'd have escaped, when we caught you you'd get another ten years. This way, you spend a night in the hot-box, Huddy gets a lashing, and y'all get out on time."

The Warden has a point and Cob doesn't dispute it.

"I'm looking out for you, Jacob Lee."

The door rattles again and the warden's voice starts moving away. "I'll send Andy out first light. I got a few things 'round the place need doing. Let the niggers worry the rocks around for a few days."

Cob pinches the ember from the cigarette, drops it into a corner, and tries to sleep.

IN SOUTHEASTERN KENTUCKY, Cob's twice-great-grandfather Elijah B. Sutter (no one knew or could remember what the "B" stood for, if anything) had hewn the town of Sutter's Mill from the forest before he sent for his wife, Esther Marie. Besides the mill and town, he raised tobacco and five sons. Two of them he buried in coffins sawn from his own trees even though, or maybe because, they had shamed him by dying to preserve an imperfect Union he didn't believe in. The sons he wished for were never born. The sons who lived wished they hadn't and left Kentucky and a father freshly buried and a mother longing to be.

Two generations plowed asunder the name Elijah Sutter every year, and the following spring, weeds would grow back and have to be hoed before they choked the cotton and peas. As soon as he was strong enough, Cob spent all summer pulling at the weed-scars of that unknown (to him) ancestor. When the bolls split open, the family would march into the cotton and snap off the tufts of livelihood and poke them into a sack that was, by rule, larger than themselves.

The first cabin Cob's father raised in Arkansas took all summer to build. As soon as the cotton was planted, John and Cob's uncle Richard had to chop logs every day for a month. They dovetailed the ends and stacked them into a precise square. Brothers and sister slept in the loft. Mother and Father slept in a straw mattress on a bed frame brought from Kentucky. A wardrobe in one corner and a cupboard in the other were the only furniture until the shake shingles went on and there was time to make chairs and a table.

Fall came sweetly over the hills and a hog would be killed and scalded then hoisted under a tripod of thick saplings. Some of the skin was flayed off and shanks carefully extracted and a fire drawn up in the smokehouse. Lard was rendered down and poured into buckets and kept in the cellar. The hams were cured and hung and smoked bacon was sliced and fried. The tangy smoke smell was tiring but preferable to nothing.

Sometimes Cob would have to shoot a dog or coyote that threatened the food, but once in a while, if it was a barely-clothed boy whose sunken chest pressed harder on Cob's heart than on the boy's, he'd offer a napkin of scraps and an apple and the boy would crouch down and eat both in front of him.

Shackled to the Lees by blood, but separated by two centuries, the Jacobys came to the Virginia colony to escape indignation and rotten vegetables thrown from nowhere. Flood and fire took the first two houses Ephrem built. The third, the largest and final, house was wrestled from the forest in 1711. His wife Meredith incanted over the farm and slaves without her husband's consent—an act which some of the slaves adored and some despised. She helped birth three variously complected generations of Jacobys and survived her husband by more years than she had been married to him.

Ephrem wrought into being an only son, Thomas Andrews Jacoby. His nurse, an octaroon favored by Ephrem and Meredith both, though for different reasons, brought him up in a tradition passed down, it's said, from John Faustus and Mephostophilis and not from his mother or the octaroon herself. His whip fell sharply and without provocation and he passed from this world through a cloud of powder smoke and willed only scars down backs and along furrows.

Soft gray light filters through the slit and along uneven edges. Cob sees the snuffed end of the cigarette floating in the bucket. He shifts the weight of the wrist shackles around. Sweat drips from his nose. He leans up to look out the slit and sees the mules stamp the ground in the corral, behind the barracks building. Swallows flit in and out of eaves and an owl marks last call before the dawn. It's still hours before the trustee comes and unlocks the door and Cob hoes tomatoes and carrots and listens to the Warden carry on about his son in law school over in Oxford and apologizes again, soggy cigar going to seed in his mouth.

Cob's mouth lusts after the side of fresh perch sizzling over a small fire and the handful of coffee boiled in a peach tin painfully abandoned the day the State of Mississippi caught up with him. Cards, gin, and country girls dazzled by automobiles and electric lights and the pages of a Sears & Roebuck not soiled and wadded and thrown into the cesspit were the only companions Cob had had since leaving Arkansas in a rotting boxcar shared with eight other men and their concomitant lice and fleas. The shark who out-bluffed him had bared his blackened and putrid teeth at the windfall, but only until Cob knocked four of them into his throat and took back his and three other's lost dignity. The shark and the three bemoaned the lost teeth and twice-lost gains and adjured appropriate punishment, the getting of which sufficed as recompense.

Instead of the hot-box, Cob thinks of the train car he would have been waking up in if he and Huddy had been drawn to replace rail ties and drive spikes instead of working the new road. He thinks of getting a job in a packing house or slaughtering hogs for three dollars a week and a hot supper and waking up early because of her, any her, snoring and rolling over and pulling a thin sheet off of him.

He looks down at his striped uniform and chuckles. The stripes get funnier and Cob laughs but his rough throat makes him cough and sputter. He thinks of drinking from the bucket, but his stomach wretches at the thought so he doesn't. He starts to hum a hymn his mother sang while picking. Though all Hell assail me, I shall not be moved, Jesus will not fail me, I shall not be moved. Just like the tree that's planted by the water, I shall not be moved.

Keys rattle at the lock and there's a snap.

The door creaks on its hinges and the morning sun rushes in and Cob is blinded. He squints and blinks at the brilliance but can trace the outline of the trustee. Cob stares at the dark figure and doesn't speak.

"Well, you gettin' out or not?" the man says. He reaches in and grabs Cob's arm and helps him scoot forward. He flips the shackles around clumsily and unlocks them. The weight comes off Cob's arms and is flung to the ground. He unlocks the leg irons and Cob tries to stretch out his legs and stand on the step but can't.

"God Almighty, Cob. Spend one night in the 'box and you can't do for yourself?"

The trustee drags Cob down the steps by the arm. He stumbles onto the grass and stops. He turns to the trustee and smiles.

"Fine morning coming on, don't you think, Andy?"

The man blows through his teeth at Cob and walks away in disgust.

SOMETIMES THE PLAGUES ARE SCHEDULED MAUREEN TOLMAN FLANNERY

Persuasion can solidify an adversary
by the very fervor of its intent to effect change.
Don't you feel it as you speak, eloquent,
full of passionate certainty, how the listener's lip
stretches tight across set teeth,
eyes firmly fixed on someplace other than your face.
And you wonder, even as your logic flows
like generations from a strong progenitor,
if it isn't God at work with His own ideas,
hardening the heart of your audience
as He did with the Pharaoh against Moses.
Pharaoh, entrenched,
hearing argument after argument,
became, with each,
more hell-bent on seeing plagues
invested upon him in due time.

AN OVERTURE'S TURN DEANNA HERSHISER

At breakfast my view is Yasmine's eaves over the back fence. Late August's straw-scent drifts through our sliding screen. Many afternoons at my clothesline I've heard Yasmine with her four kids in the yard. Their forgotten toys will face a sodden October.

I lift a prayer for her and pour enriched grains into a bowl. Bible open near my elbow, I read my usual chapter a day. When I'm done Yasmine's voice rises, sharp, from her back porch, answered in kind by her mother's. Her mother is visiting from New York, trying to get Yasmine's life in order.

I'm sure I should do something. Walk to the fence and say good morning, maybe. I decide instead to start the washer.

We met nearly a year ago because I carried her a basket. New people make me uncomfortable, but I took to heart admonitions from our church leaders. The Sunday before, Pastor Greg had summed up by asking, "Don't you *long* to be effective for God in your lifetime?"

Yasmine's family had just moved into the house around the block. The former owner, whose kids had played with mine now and then, told me about the buyers. "Worthless," she said. "The girl's parents bought the place. She's pregnant with her fourth, never been married."

Yasmine, her navel visible through her shirt, accepted my gifts—tea, a mug, floral notecards—and cleared space for me on the sofa. Two boys and a delicate girl played in foothills of toys near boxes stacked to the ceiling.

"Things are crazy around here," Yasmine said. "We're waiting for a ride to the drop-in nursery." Her youngest toddled over and clung to her leg. She hoisted him to her breast. "He's named Noah, because their father, Michael, and I were setting out for new horizons, a voyage into the unknown, the Oregon Trail. Michael will be back for this next one's birth, I think." She sighed. "He has issues."

I had to admit I liked her wide smile, her unassuming brown eyes.

"I can't drive," Yasmine went on. "Seizures.

And I won't take medication now." She laughed. "Probably not after the baby, either. I can't live in more of a haze than I do!"

My two kids at home computed, studied, invented. They were a little older than hers. We home-schooled. I told Yasmine goodbye and returned around the block to them, a small, satisfied bounce in my stride.

The next week Yasmine phoned to ask about our neighborhood pool's evening swim lessons starting soon. "If you could drive us over," she said, "I'll pay for your kids, too. Mom and Papa have loaned me some to keep us healthy—I'm paying it back—and it would help so much if you'd look after Celestia in the pool."

Seven wedged into my little Ford that first Monday, rolled-up towels snug in the trunk, the children hesitant during the six block ride to the pool and rec center.

Yasmine looked unsteady in a light blue suit at the shallow end. The steamed and darkened windows rose behind, her belly swelled in front. My chlorine breaths puffed motor-boat bubbles for delicate Celestia, who giggled and splashed. Yasmine floated and coaxed little Noah. Our older children were in groups according to age and ability, their teachers' voices echoing humidly off cement walls.

Guiding Celestia to the pool's edge when we were finished I saw Yasmine climb out, stumble, then stand, head bowed. Currents of dripping students surged past, frilled pink, aqua, titanium-sheened, bare feet and knobby knees. Yasmine regained equilibrium and I breathed.

Heart pounding, I caught up to her in the dressing room. "What do I do if I'm around when you start . . . um . . . seizing?"

Yasmine laughed. "Just let me go down, hold my head, give me air. It'll probably be worse for you than for me. Anyway, it doesn't happen often."

I dreamed of Yasmine in labor that night. "Breathe," I said, cradling her head. "Just breathe." She couldn't. Her hands shook, fingers clawlike. I'd seen the same thing once on PBS. The pressure of her neck trying to arch backward was tremendous. What if she swallowed her tongue? "Help!" I called. Tim woke then and held me as the panic subsided.

Near Thanksgiving Yasmine and the baby did fine, Michael and her mother both on hand, when the newest little boy made his entrance into their lives.

TODAY I ANSWER THE DOORBELL close to four o'clock. It's Yasmine and Celestia. The afternoon has warmed as much as expected. "We walked to Burger King," Celestia announces, "and now we're thirsty."

As I pour lemonade Yasmine explains, "I needed a break. My mom . . ." A hand cradles her forehead in weary salute. "Well. Michael and Mom hope to organize my life, and we are . . . negotiating."

Since last year I've learned something of Yasmine's view regarding order. Not that we've been fully in each other's lives. Michael remained with Yasmine once the baby came, taking fatherhood more seriously, finding work here and there.

IN FEBRUARY I SHOWED YASMINE a catalog of educational toys and books, and she ordered some things for her kids. The evening I walked over to deliver her order, Yasmine came to the front door toweling her hair.

"You got a haircut," I said as Yasmine steered me between piles to a kitchen chair. The clothes dryer droned from the hall.

Yasmine nodded. "We've had a horrible week," she said, spooning up food for her high-chair-bound youngest son. He launched into impatient animation of each limb, saying, "Ap, ap!"

I noted letters scrawled on the highest cupboard doors. In crayon, maybe. Trying to make out what they said—Embrace the Chaos, I decided—I missed what Yasmine was talking about. The children, their friends, their school, then, "head lice." My muscles froze.

"I've run everything through the drier, and bathed the kids, and used the shampoo, and cut our hair. So it better be taken care of. But I'm so tired." She kept spooning for little ap-boy. I tried to bring forth a sound of sympathy, while resisting an urge to scratch. To flee.

Back at home I showered. Tim said I was silly. My head itched for days.

An Easter cantata was in the works at church, and I planned to ask Yasmine to come. She loved music, and the choir Tim and I sang in was pretty good. Mainly, though, I wanted Yasmine and the message to connect. As it turned out, Pastor Greg concluded the service with a beautiful altar call. We who looked down from the stage watched three people make their way forward to accept Christ as their Savior.

Not Yasmine, though. I really meant to invite her. I thought of it driving home the week beforehand. Turning onto her street, I saw the oldest boy out front lobbing a ball against the house, and Michael stepping off the porch. He yelled something over his shoulder before swigging his bottle of beer. Slowing the car, I readied a smile in case I caught Michael's glance.

The boy stood still a moment, scratching the back of his head.

Prickles assaulted my scalp. I accelerated, planning to call later.

Near the end of the cantata I thought about Yasmine and knew silly fears had caused my failure. I began praying for another chance.

OUR WINDOW AIR CONDITIONER shudders alive when I flip its switch. I join Yasmine and Celestia at the table. My kids are down the block, using up precious summer moments with friends before they hit the books again next week.

Yasmine presses her glass against her cheek.

I ask, "How long will your mother stay?"

She shrugs. "I agreed with Mom and Michael's plan to have the floors redone," she says, resigned. "The guys will come tomorrow. Today over there Mom's tossing everything onto the patio and sorting for a garage sale." She leans back in the chair. "Who knows? Maybe I'll earn something toward school."

"Oh?" I brush off crumbs my son left behind.

"Yes, I think I'll register for a university class," Yasmine says. "Music theory. I'd almost finished it in New York, before we left."

"Mommy." Celestia tugs the shoulder-piece of Yasmine's loose tank top. "Mommy, you can't let Grandma take me away on the plane."

Yasmine laughs, leans in close to her. "You think I would let that happen?" She explains her mother's idea to have Celestia in a posh pre-school back East. "There's no negotiating some things," she concludes. "We're on opposite sides of the country in more ways than one. Hey, I may have this to deal with—" she taps her head, her voice in crescendo—"but Mom's got to learn she can't dictate my whole life."

As Yasmine speaks, my mind analyzes options. This could be a chance to say something of consequence. I tried one other time with

Yasmine, back in June, but it didn't turn out too well. Not too badly, maybe. Maybe it was meant to lead to this moment.

IN JUNE, I WALKED WITH YASMINE to the park one Saturday, the kids capering around us, baby apping in his stroller. Yasmine's home had been lice-free for weeks. That morning, though, she and Michael had duked it out verbally in the front yard, while neighbors trimmed hedges and mulched rose bushes. Her eyes like a battle-worn soldier's, she told me, "Everything's too much right now."

Though I strolled calmly beside Yasmine, inside I resembled the chestnut mare my daughter sometimes got to ride at our friends' farm—saddled and eager to perform. "You know," I said, finding my opening, "there was a time I felt that way, before Tim and I had kids. We reached rock-bottom in our marriage."

Yasmine, holding Noah's hand, glanced at me sideways.

"Oh, lots of things contributed, not just him, not just me. But through it all I discovered there is someone who'll never let me down."

"You mean Tim?"

"Everyone on earth eventually disappoints us."

"Huh?"

"The one who's never failed me is Jesus."

We reached the park. "Look both ways!" Yasmine commanded, and we all crossed to the playground. Our feet sank slightly into a fragrant wood chip carpet. I watched the baby from a bench while Yasmine pushed Noah's swing. My thoughts skittered as clouds built up in the west.

Later Yasmine nursed her youngest, the others busy in the sandbox. I examined my thumbs, not sure how to continue.

"I guess I'm disappointed," Yasmine said.

"Why?"

"What you said, about Jesus. I hoped you were telling me how you and Tim found ideal love."

"We did, because the Lord—well. There've been hard times, even with the Lord's help. I'm just saying nothing's ideal, except a relationship with God."

"Ha!" Yasmine crossed her legs and stroked her baby's cheek. "Excuse me, Deanna, I just haven't experienced God that way. My parents? From day one, it was go to church, put on your best, show everyone how fake you can be. At home, violence and all kinds of shit is fine, then at church you pretend it never happened. No thanks."

"Oh. I'm sorry."

"Then, this morning. You know those neighbors across the street to the right?"

I'd never met them.

"When we first moved in, she comes over, all smiles. We talked nearly every day. I actually considered visiting their church. After Michael came back, one day she's asking questions, wondering what he does for a living. I mention he's trying to straighten out. 'Well, so, you mean your parents support you?' she says. I say, 'Not much; we get some assistance.' 'You're on Welfare?!' she asks, like I'd just told her I had the plague. After that she avoids me, my children, the gravel in front of my house."

I said nothing.

"This morning, Michael is letting me have it with how bad a mother I am, how irresponsible, like he can talk. I tell him to go; we don't need this. My neighbor, outside with her husband, calls from where she's working behind her roses. 'You both need help,' she says. 'Go inside and pick up the phone. We're trying to be productive here.'"

I blustered. "What a—how could she?"

"Well, it's just life," Yasmine said. "I'm thinking it's time to move on again."

The sky darkened. To tympanic rumbles we gathered children, headed home. In the back yard I snatched dripping socks off the line.

That evening I did step aerobics in our living room. Tim had found the step at a yard sale so I needn't pay fitness center dues once I learned the moves. He'd bought me bouncy music and given me space. Tonight my workout included lots of power punches.

As my side leaps slowed, I formed another plan. I'd show Yasmine there was one Christian who cared.

"Hello?" Yasmine's voice on the phone was faint.

"Sorry, did I wake you?"

"No. I'm feeling lonely. Michael's off somewhere."

Water sloshed. She must be in the tub. The only time and space to relax, she'd told me, bathing after nightfall.

"Don't move away," I said. "Please. I really want you to stay."

Now Yasmine smiles politely. They've finished their lemonade. I've opened my mouth but failed to summon any nuggets of wisdom to finally start Yasmine pondering her need for God.

"I'd better get home," she says, and to Celestia, "Come on, Honey." Nothing passes my lips but a lame goodbye.

After ten o' clock, I settle down to watch TV with Tim. Voices carry across the back lawns, rising. Most words are unclear. Michael and the mother alternately implore, exclaim. Yasmine curses, weeps. Finally crickets take back the night.

The next Thursday as I finish work at my computer then dishes in the kitchen, I'm thinking. Not exactly plotting. I pick up the phone.

"Yasmine?"

"Oh, hello." She sounds good. Rested, maybe. Her floors got finished—they look nice, I'll have to see them, and her mother's gone back to New York, alone.

"There's this thing at my church. Saturday morning. It's when we sign up for . . . well, things to do with women's . . . issues. For support and all." I fumble, thinking I make it sound more like a social service forum than the flowery invitation it will be to a range of Bible studies and potlucks. But this slant seems to impress Yasmine.

"Okay," she says. "I think I'd like that. I'll take all the support I can get."

"Great. I can pick you up at 9:45." It's going so well that I feel deceitful. Then I remember something else. "Would you like a zucchini?"

Our garden produces dozens; I often forget to pick them until they resemble green-striped whalings. But Yasmine has accepted them before, claiming she likes any size. "You can't find stuff like this in New York," she says.

We meet at the back fence. Through its slats I see she's still robed and slippered. Celestia follows along, toting some books. "These are kind of old for my kids," Yasmine says. "I thought you might use them in your lessons for now."

We trade offerings across the weathered boards, shaded by rogue maples shooting up too close to our rhododendron—ten-foot adolescents snickering behind emerald leaf-fingers. I avoid a large spider's web.

"Well, see you Saturday," says Yasmine, turning to go. Celestia is tugging her toward breakfast.

"I'll look at your floors then," I call after her.

Yasmine stops and turns back, lifting her free hand. "Thank you for caring about me."

I GET READY IN GOOD TIME two mornings later and decide to risk landing at Yasmine's house a few minutes early. Last night I tried calling to remind her but got no answer. Now I imagine a house full of sleeping people, my knock waking Michael. I can wait, though, while Yasmine pulls on an outfit. I promise myself I won't worry or fidget. This will be fun, and Yasmine will find support from the ladies, if not in exactly the way she expects.

No one at Yasmine's answers my first, short knock. I keep my momentum and don't give up. My ears strain for fumbling sounds inside and finally hear them. Michael stands there, head bowed. He's fully dressed. The hardwood floor gleams behind him, sunlight an extended wave beneath the lonely sofa. Yasmine's mother's garage sale left things pretty sparse.

"Sorry if I—" As I speak Michael raises his head. His eyes are depths of weariness. "Is Yasmine here?"

He pushes open the screen. "Yasmine's dead."

He invites me in, sits with me on the sofa. Explains it was a seizure Thursday night during Yasmine's bath. He'd kissed the children, left for the evening. He didn't return until morning.

For some reason, after stopping at home, I go on to the women's brunch. Support. That's what Yasmine wanted to find there. It's weird, trying to decide what to do with my mouth. My lips feel like worms stretched across my upper chin. Seeing Pastor Greg's wife, Janene, off to the side before the program starts, I tell her.

"Was that the woman who drowned in her bathtub? Oh, I read it in the paper this morning. So awful; her daughter found her." Janene places a hand on my arm.

"She had epilepsy," I say, stupid worms not forming syllables well. "She was coming, today, as my guest."

"Oh, Honey, I'm so sorry. You've made requests for her all along, haven't you? Been working with her. We'll stop for prayer this moment."

Janene walks to the platform and explains into the mic what's happened. The women bow their heads. "Dear Lord," she says, "this a difficult shock. Thank you that Deanna's friend is in heaven right now."

I stiffen. My intertwined fingers pulse. I don't know what I expected. A teary pronouncement, if not a rending of clothes. In this room I learned that if the unsaved don't say the right words, if they miss accepting Jesus, heaven will not happen.

I open my eyes. A hundred or so decked-out women whisper "Amen" from their seats around decorated tables. They smile as recorded music swells and the performance commences.

FROM OUR BACK PORCH IN TWILIGHT, I make out the line of Yasmine's roof above the trees. Clouds obscure most stars; the breeze is turning cold. I huddle on the wooden bench, knees up under my chin.

The day before the funeral, most of the neighbors gathers at Yasmine's house bearing food. Her parents stand by, expressions of thanks in their quavering eyes. "I told Yasmine not to bathe when Michael wasn't here," her mother confids to me. "She lived without thinking, you know?"

As we nibbled finger sandwiches, Michael tells me about Yasmine's last supper. "She really liked the zucchini," he said.

I avoid speaking with the rose bush woman from across the street.

Yasmine's service is closed-casket. Graveside. People speak in turns, shaded from harsh sunlight by a striped awning. A social services woman from the drop-in nursery. Her oldest son, reading a poem he composed last Mother's Day.

I try not to imagine her body inside the box. I don't want to think of Celestia's vain attempts to wake her in the tub.

Thank you for caring about me.

I imagine my own moves that Thursday night. A trajectory to Yasmine's bathroom, past sliding door and garden, over troublesome maples, faded fence, her unkempt yard. While Yasmine settled into soothing water, moisture formed on my brow. My arms did power punches, ponytail bobbing as I worked the plastic step. As my heart rate climbed, Yasmine's hands began to shake.

Tim has assured me I did the best I knew how. What more could I, as a Christian friend, have done?

I stand up and leave through the gate. Walking around the block, I shiver.

Lately my prayers are different. My disciplines slide. I worry sometimes I risk stepping into chaos.

In front of the empty house with the "For Sale" sign out front I stop. Yasmine's children flew back East with her mother. I haven't heard what became of Michael. My hands cover my face when the sobs begin.

At home again in my room, knees protesting hardwood beside my bed, I wait. For questions, maybe.

GOODBYE SOPHIE DON HOESEL

THERE IS A DICHOTOMOUS CLEANSING that comes from the flowing of blood. It stains—the blood stains. Shirts, carpets, women, walls, guitar strings. Bleed enough, play for hours in countless venues, in buses on nameless highways, and in room thirty-two in a thousand hotel rooms, and the strings will hold the hue, tinged pink beneath the stage lights. When the gels are red, the spots bathing me in nether worldly luminance, the taut phosphor lines beneath my fingers vibrate with a subdued intensity, sharing a color camaraderie with the lanterns hung from the ceiling of whatever aged venue I'm in. The red light is supposed to make the experience something ethereal for the audience, draw them in, cause them to lean forward in their seats, pull them into each note I coax from the Lowden, but in the dark they look like specters coming out of midnight, eyes ablaze, a psychic devouring of my flesh. I'm viscerally naked, and I'm high, and I play to keep the ghosts at bay, keep them in their seats. What sates them is the music pulled from the roiling place in my stomach, something I can't fake. I can't play from fear alone; what I pull from the guitar must be something that needs its release, and they would know the difference. The music is hook and fence. It is also silence, or it produces silence, an anticipation that might as well be a vacuum, and my notes fill it, and the specters breathe it, their chests rising and falling with the tones, my voice. My eyes are closed, and the specters are there, and the roiling thing pours out, hook and fence.

It's an old Irish song, a ditty from centuries gone, and it's fresh and relevant and the specters love it because it's a rediscovery. They know every word, and some of them are singing along, as men would have in a tavern a hundred years before the Magna Carta. Calloused fingers play over the strings, framing the open tuning, harnessing dissonance. Bartok in strings.

It's dichotomous because, while it stains what it touches, it's also a cleansing. Bleeding releases toxins from the body. It removes what we can't process. When we bleed we expel demons. I've sometimes wondered if the Lowden harbors demons; if it does, they are monsters of my own making, my private fluids.

I smell the old upholstery of the seats. It's an odor sickening and sweet at the same time; it anchors me to the here and now, and it forces its way into my throat like rape. My foot taps the wood floor of the stage in time to the music, an off-tempo, and they watch because they know the rhythm, celebrate the fact that their head nods will sync with something besides their own internal metronome, and because they hunger for a connection that I can't acknowledge from up here. I know that my music means something different for everyone, that many of them think they share with me an epiphany of soul or experience that caused me to pen a lyric or hammer through a bar. I wonder what they would think if they knew that I sometimes can't remember why I wrote a song.

I answered an e-mail once, from someone who asked me if I had done a studio session with an artist in the early eighties. I told him that I couldn't remember. I can't. So much from those years runs together. There are whole portions of time that are blurred to the point that I can't extract anything meaningful from the experiential conglomeration. A piece of a show in Des Moines, an art festival in Cambridge, a thing that might have been an album release party in London, a marriage. It wasn't drugs. I didn't do that back then; I seldom indulge now. It's just that if one does something long enough—lives and breathes a singular purpose for three decades—there are simply things that won't stick when thrown against the cerebral flytrap.

I hear my voice pouring out into the hot mic. It's rough but it's real, and I'm singing this song as if for the first time, with all of its lyrical morbidity, and the words come without conscious thought because I've done this one at least a thousand times. And the only way I can bring it to the people who paid to hear me is to forget that I've ever sang it, to pull from a generic emotional pool—because I can't remember when I first heard it, or why I decided to add it to my show.

It's the second song in the encore and, as it finishes, as the final notes hold solid form so that I think I can see F-sharp floating over some heads in the front row, there is a half-second of silence before the five-hundred bodies belonging to the five-hundred heads stand and bring their hands together in a dualistic ritual: a lingering honor crafted from the knowledge that they have shared in something for which few superlatives are adequate, and the hope that I will play just one more. I won't, and I pull the cord from the base of the Lowden and carry it off the stage with me.

A line of red is flowing down my pointer finger, where the first string caught me after it snapped. I feel good about having been able to adjust the song, to spread the notes over the remaining strings so that only the keenest of observers would have ever caught the difference. I put the finger in my mouth and suck at the blood.

My tour manager is waiting for me as I step out of view of the crowd. I hand Lars the guitar and he claps me on the shoulder as I walk by. He's like a gnome, short and thick and connected by some invisible string to the earth. I'm through the door without a word, leaving him to wipe the sweat from the Lowden and replace the string before it goes back in its case. I'm in a narrow, dimly lit hallway, with three doors opening into what pass for dressing rooms, although one of these is stuffed full of period clothing that looks to have been lifted from the cast of a Dickens play. *What's today, my fine fellow?* I think it's Tuesday. The room they gave me is the last in the line, and it's fine as far as rooms go. It has a chair, a small refrigerator, a card table, and a coat hook, and I've never needed much more than these. On the card table is a bucket holding the three remaining bottles of water. I lift one from the mostly-melted ice, twist off the cap and drink as water runs down to my wrist and seeps into my shirtsleeve.

I sit, holding the half-empty bottle on my thigh, and let myself sink into the hard wood of the much-abused chair. For a full minute I let my eyes focus on nothing, allowing the unnatural phenomenon that is stage lighting to release its grip. I'm not sure how much time passes before I realize that I'm looking at a calendar on the opposite wall, but I think I've been tracing the lines of the cubist painting that adorns the upper section for a good while. In the bottom right corner is the name of the venue, the Carlton Theatre. In Greensboro. I'm in Greensboro.

"We're in Greensboro," I say to Lars, who has just appeared in the doorway.

"That explains a lot. I thought it was a little too quiet to be Detroit."

Lars has been with me for eleven years, during which he's failed at two marriages, sired three children, and lost his oldest daughter—a college sophomore—in a car wreck in Brussels. I believe I'm the most constant thing in his life and, for some reason, thinking about that makes me sad.

"How's the guitar?"

"Restrung and sleeping like a baby."

Sophie. She was a cellist. A Mercedes crossed the line and hit her head on. We were in San Francisco when Lars got the call.

"The guys are packing out. We're staying at the Hilton. You want me to run you over there?"

"I'm hungry."

"That's what room service is for."

She would have been famous. When she was eighteen, the summer before she started college, I invited her to the studio where we laid down three tracks for my new album. What she coaxed from her instrument haunts me.

"I don't think room service will cut it tonight."

Lars runs a hand through the thick white beard that he's cultivated with a botanist's intensity since I've known him.

"There's not much in Greensboro after eleven."

"Is it after eleven?"

"There's a three-star with Continental American, and a dance club at which you would single-handedly double the average age of the patrons."

"And I pay you because?"

"I make a mean omelet."

Every time one of those songs is played, Lars and his family get a nickel.

"I think I'm just going to walk for a while."

This is the point at which most tour managers would do everything but block the door with their bodies, and Lars is amply supplied in that area. Their bread and butter consists of their charges performing as many shows as logistically possible in the shortest amount of time; arraignments and drunk tanks seldom make positive contributions toward that end goal. In our case, this is one of those instances in which familiarity bequeaths a studied fatalism.

"We're out at 6 a.m.," Lars says.

I HAVE A SPOT AT THE BAR, a freak of happenstance if ever I've seen one. When I arrived, I fought for the attention of a lovely and supple young bartender who seemed rather put out with having to wait on a man for whom she assumed her feminine wiles would have only a marginal effect on her tip percentage. If only she knew how age can enhance one's appreciation of nubile beauty.

I'm the oldest person in the building.

It's not a hypothesis, nor self-deprecation. It's fact. Every person I see is a vibrant youngster—the thing I pretend to be, the skin the crowd lends me. The guy checking IDs at the door gave me a twice over before waving me through.

I'm nursing a Maker's, my second. And I'm just starting to enter that place where the edge is dulled a fraction, where I can set roots into the bar stool and begin to enjoy my surroundings. I don't think a person can really experience a place like this without surrendering a part of himself. There is too much stimuli to process, too many physical and emotional eddies of which to keep track, and I doubt an air-traffic controller, suitably equipped with a device that monitors young psyches, could keep them all from colliding.

There's an anonymity in a place like this that I welcome, even if I don't have much need for it. I'm not famous enough—at least not in the right circles—to have to worry about autograph seekers and hangers on. I like to think my fans are more cerebral, the sorts with which I could have a drink, exchange a pleasantry or two, and then wish them well as they travel back to wherever it is they came from. In some cities, more than half of the audience comes from somewhere else. Tonight there were some from Nashville, from Atlanta, even from as far away as St. Louis. Which is insane because I'll be in St. Louis this weekend. I'm certain they'll be at that show, too.

Dance music is pounding down from the ceiling through high-end speakers that haven't been properly calibrated. Like serving a meal on fine China that's been polished with a pumice stone. I do not have a bias against club music. It has a purpose, and every once in a while there's a real gem, something that stretches the limits of the genre, or pulls something foreign and lovely into the mix. The people around me seem to enjoy it, or ignore it. Bars are seldom about music; they're seldom even about alcohol.

A space opens up beside me and is filled again before I can blink. A lovely brunette with pale features and thick lashes. She gives me a half-smile as she settles in, tossing a casual wave to someone over my right shoulder. She places a purse on the bar and my eyes follow her hand as it rummages through the contents and emerges with a pack of cigarettes. Her fingers are marvelous, long and narrow and a white bordering on ghostly. Short fingernails. She lights up, draws her lungs full, then waves for the bartender.

"Cabernet and a Maker's neat."

I enjoy a private smile and then drain my glass.

By the time my next drink arrives, I'm forgetting the woman next to me. It's something of a gift to have a mind that releases things easily, that slips into free association like a computer screen saver. There's also something to be said about appreciating beauty in small doses, looking away before familiarity can ruin the moment. DeLillo might have written something along those lines. I think he did.

She draws me back.

"Nice set tonight."

She's wearing dark jeans and a black sweater, and has a hand around the highball glass, an easy grip. The wine glass sits near but, at the moment, it's an afterthought.

"Thanks."

"The last one, especially. Broken string and all."

I swivel on the stool, pulled into the conversation by both the subject matter and her manner. She's not hitting on me, nor does she give off the vibe of some of my longtime fans. This is easy conversation, a meeting of contemporaries separated by perhaps twenty-five years.

I hold up my finger, showing her the gash along the side that is only now setting with a proper clot.

"No matter how nicely you treat a guitar, sometimes it bites back."

"Instinct," she says, leaning over to study the wound. "How old is it?"

"The finger? Same age as the rest of me."

"The Lowden," she says with a smile.

"The lady knows her guitars. I bought it in 1986, which makes it twenty-one years old."

She nods and takes a drink. After she lowers the glass, she gives me a wink.

"I would have been six when you bought it."

"The eighties was a horrible decade to have been born into, but it looks like you came out of it well enough. Do you play?"

"I dabble."

"With what?"

"A Gretsch Dreadnought."

"Expensive taste for a dabbler."

She shrugs.

"I like nice things."

Then she raises the whiskey and drains the last swallow. She sets the empty glass at the far edge of the bar and moves the wine to the head of the class.

"Whiskey and wine?"

She gives the glass a slight swirl. "Body and blood."

"Corpus et sanguis."

"Catholic school?" she asks with mild surprise.

"The benefits of a classical education."

She lifts the glass, sets her lips on the edge as a priest would. "Deo gratias," she says before taking a small sip.

"Amen."

She laughs, and it's a sound pure enough to drive away the residual influence of the specters.

"What's your name?"

"Monica," she answers.

MONICA'S FINGERS PLAY over the Gretsch's strings, and her left hand dances on the frets with accuracy and passion. She lied to me; she's more than a dabbler. Much more. She holds the pick in two fingers, easing out a melody, while the other digits provide punch and counterpunch. Off-rhythm and just as natural as you please.

It's one of mine, a piece I seldom perform live, except when I'm feeling particularly nostalgic. She nails every note, every change, even the emotion of the song. And she does it with her eyes on mine, competent and warm and maybe watching for my reaction.

She sits on the trunk of her Acura. It's gray, the interior is leather, it has a sunroof, and there's a UNC decal affixed to the rear window. And the backseat is filled with clothes and books and food.

Her playing enraptures me, and it's not because of her obvious technical skill. Many of my songs are difficult, requiring exacting technique, but a good studio musician can mimic me with practice. No, it's the knowledge that she's nailed the back-story behind the piece. She plays it as if she's lived the life behind it.

I wish I had the Lowden, so that I could sit next to her, feel the car sink under our combined weight, and play along. Instead I watch, enjoying the moment as if I had not written the song, as if it belongs to her. And she returns it to me as a gift.

When she finishes, and the last notes scatter to the breeze, it's appropriate that I clap, and I do so with the same appreciation those who applaud me feel. She smiles and looks down.

"You're remarkable," I say as I join her at the car, leaning against it.

"Thanks. I had a good teacher."

"Keep talking like that and you'll swell my ego."

"Why? I wasn't referring to you."

I must appear more chagrined than I imagine because she takes one look at my face and laughs.

"I studied under Jordan Moorehouse," she says once she regains her composure.

"You went to Edenton?"

"For a year or so."

Her answer catches me by surprise. Edenton is more exclusive than Julliard. They take only the very best. When you are accepted at Edenton you are there for the duration. Anything else is professional suicide.

"Why did you leave?"

She shrugs. "I didn't need it anymore."

"Isn't that rather arrogant?"

"You didn't attend and you turned out alright."

"When I was your age, they wouldn't have let me near the place."

We are a hundred yards from the club, and I can hear the music crossing the distance as something like white noise, just an insistent base pulse. Occasionally, a patron will enter or exit but, beyond these, Monica and I are alone. The street is quiet, I haven't seen a car pass since we've been out here, and the night is approaching crisp, the kind of air that makes each individual nostril hair tingle. It's the air we had in London when I was a boy, and it makes me feel younger.

"Do you live out of your car?"

"That's a funny thing to ask."

"You seem to have most of your worldly possessions in your back seat."

"It's convenient."

"What if you need a shirt pressed?"

"Then I press it."

I nod as if I understand. And I suppose that, in a way, I do. Who am I to question a person about their living arrangements when I go for months at a time living out of suitcases and never having the same pillow? When I was younger, when the touring thing was new, I would haul my own pillow around, working on the proposition that as long as I had that one constant, I would never feel wholly out of sorts. It only took me leaving a half-dozen of them behind over the course of a year, and having to cope with the resultant disappointment, to cause me to quit the practice. A vague discomfort is less disconcerting than an acute sense of loss.

"Do you play out?"

She answers with a headshake. "This is the first time in more than a year that I've played for anyone."

"That's almost a crime."

"Do you want to take a walk?"

Without waiting for an answer, she hops down, pops the trunk, and sets the Gretsch in its case.

Greensboro is an oddly quiet city at night. During the day, there is a sense of industry and purpose and normalcy that pervades it, even if the city center is small enough to seem like one of those towns that pops up from nowhere in the Old West. But after the sun goes down, it's like a string of Christmas lights with only a few working bulbs. People gather around these hot spots, leaving the rest of the city barren. It's one of these sections we're in now, like walking through a Hollywood set after shooting has wrapped.

Monica sets the pace, and she seems happy to stroll. And I'm content to let her lead. I'm not certain I know what this night is about, why I'm walking around with a woman half my age when the bus will be pulling out in less than five hours. I'm not much of a womanizer, at least not for the last few years, and while she is simply stunning, I'm attuned to the ephemeral nature of things enough to understand that something other than lechery directs me.

"Why did you quit Edenton?"

"Why did you get divorced?"

"Which time?"

"The first and third. Your second wife deserved it."

"If only the judge had been inclined to see things your way."

"Not everyone can be so forward thinking."

We reach an intersection and an El Camino is idling at a red light. I see the other light cycle through the yellow and then to red, and Monica and I wait while the car accelerates past.

"How do you decide what to write about?" she asks.

"That's not really the right question. It's more about deciding what I won't write about."

She digests this for a few moments before replying.

"So what won't you write about?"

"Very little." When she doesn't answer, I elaborate. "It's dishonest to ignore the ugly parts of humanity."

"What if there's too much ugly?"

"There's no 'what if' about it. There is too much of it."

That seems to satisfy her and we walk for a while sharing the silence, the stillness of a city with a museum quality. She makes a right turn that catches me off guard but I correct and follow. As I catch up, I see a hint of a smile on her face.

"Nashville tomorrow?"

"That's what I've been told. Will I see you there?"

"Why spoil a perfect evening with an inadequate follow-up?"

I'm not sure why, when the comment has a sharp edge, but it elicits a laugh.

"Darling, you've just recited the theme for a substantial portion of my life."

That seems to please her and, right now, that's enough for me.

Just as I'm about to say something clever, in that dry, clipped manner that only a Brit can really master, a coughing fit hits her. It begins as a clearing of the throat but quickly takes over her shoulders, her chest. It's one of those coughs that sits somewhere deep inside a person, mostly dormant, but that awakens every so often to remind its host that it's there. She brings her hand up to cover her mouth, and turns her body away until she's facing the worn brick of the building next to us. I'm caught in an odd place because, while I've come to recognize something of a kindred spirit in this woman, we are essentially strangers.

I mean to put my hand on her shoulder but it ends up around her waist, and I am leaning in close. She does not pull away but settles against me for a moment that seems fragile and fleeting. Then the coughing subsides almost as quickly as it began, and she pushes away.

"Are you alright?"

She nods and pulls a handkerchief from her front pocket, which she uses to dab at her lips. It happens quickly but, before she can ball it up and scrunch it back into the pocket, I think I see a hint of red against the white.

"Just a cold," she says in a voice made husky by the episode. Then, as if to change the subject, she slips her hand in mine and starts off again. Lecher that I am, I acquiesce to the misdirection.

Her hand is small and warm, and I can't help but enjoy the way it feels. I allow myself to be led down the streets of a city that might as well be Bangkok for the dearth of things that are familiar to me. There is an element of trust involved in letting a stranger guide you.

Up ahead I see a few lights that come into sharper focus as we walk. As time passes, they separate into a trio of hotel monikers.

"Why don't you write about death?"

The question comes from nowhere, incongruent with the mood that I've manufactured.

"I do. A good portion of my catalog is filled with it."

I feel her hand tense and have a sudden fear that she will pull it away, but it remains entwined with mine.

"You dance around it. True, people die in your songs but you've never chased their souls anywhere. You weave these brilliant lyrics around the circumstances that led to their deaths, even the occasional moral lesson to be learned, but I've never once heard you address what comes next."

"I suppose that's not really my thing."

"Isn't it one of the ugly parts of humanity that you don't ignore?"

"Touché."

It happens too quickly that we're standing in front of the Hilton. Neon and faux-stucco.

"You have to leave early," she says.

And I don't know what to say. There's a part of me that has no intention of going anywhere, that wants nothing other than to stand here with this woman, our hands touching, and let the sun rise. But there's a part of me that understands, and it wants to run.

"How long?"

She smiles and places a finger on my lips.

"What did I say about inadequate follow-ups?"

She leans close and kisses me on my grizzled, bearded cheek, lingering so that I think I might catch her up and hold her against my body. A moment later, she's gone, turning and walking away without another word. I'm rooted to the spot, watching until she disappears into the dark, negotiating loss in a way in which I've never experienced it, frightened that I'm grateful for the opportunity.

Morning is a sly animal, creeping ever so quietly.

THE MATING HABITS OF LIZARDS ANGIE POOLE

SWEETHEART, DON'T BE STUPID LIKE ME. Do everything your teachers tell you to do whether it makes sense or not. Remember that time when you were in the third grade and you asked me to help you study for that science test and you kept saying, "Earth's crust?" and I got so mad that I told you to just go to bed so that you could get up early to fail? What kind of woman says that to her kid? If I had it to do over again right now, we'd stay up all night so that you'd get you a good grade.

How can you already be thirteen? I hated that year, flat-chest, hand-me-downs, all elbows and hair spray. Spent the whole time trying to get people to like me, trying to fit in. Never did. There was this one teacher—when I ran for cheerleader—that tried to get me to go up to the other kids and just ask them to vote for me. That sounded so lame. She acted like it didn't matter where my daddy worked or which side of town we lived on. Now I see what she was getting at. Should've paid more attention in her class, got good grades, maybe made something of myself. Well, something else.

Today, the first three job applications I filled out I was honest and checked the *yes* box on the have you ever been convicted of a felony part. Then I had to watch these ~~fat-assed~~ women with no teeth and cheap Wal-Mart tennis shoes sneer at me and say their supervisors would call after they'd had a chance to look over my applications. By the time I got to the last place—a company that sells used arcade games and slot machines—I'd caught enough snap to leave that part blank, like I'd forgot to answer or something. While this greasy man looked over my paperwork, I watched a lizard shed his old skin on a shrub outside the window, like he was peeling off white pantyhose with his mouth. The guy interviewing me cleared his throat and when I looked back at him his gaze had dropped down the front of my blouse. I knew right then I was hired. Paul's saline investment paid off, huh?

My defense lawyer said Paul's new wife was pregnant at his trial. I wish I'd been acquitted. He never was going to tell his parents the truth about you or marry me.

Did Mama tell you I tried to call again? She didn't accept the charges so I'm going to use my first paycheck to get my cell phone turned back on.

My landlady, Delores, is calling me down to supper so I gotta go. Her son Pablo's girlfriend, Annie, made something called a frittata. You should see the tattoo he did on her leg. It's of the Virgin Mary and is pretty good. Tonight's my turn to do the dishes so I'll have to write again tomorrow night to tell you how the first day at my new job goes.

Wish me luck.

ALICE, MY NEW BOSS, ALREADY HATES ME. (Her husband is the owner that stares down my shirt.) She showed me how to file vendor invoices into the file cabinets and I spent the morning singing the ABC song to myself and wondering if she'd come behind me to see if I knew how to spell, if I didn't die first of blood loss from the paper cuts. I bet they haven't filed in six months. Why didn't I go to college?

At noon I carried the *taco al carbon* that Pablo made me to the lunch room. This one girl smiled my way but she didn't ask me to sit with her so I read a book Annie loaned me out by myself in the smoking area, behind the owner's office. There's this little cinderblock retaining wall on the backside of the picnic table and part of the time I watched that lizard puffing out his red throat, trying to impress another dinky little lizard. But she just ran off.

The book was pretty good—about this lady who sings church songs and takes anti-depressants but doesn't tell her preacher husband that she can't stop being sad all the time. Guess everybody has a secret. I don't want to be that way with you because anything worth hiding can't be good. So I'm going to tell you everything. You can tell me anything too. I promise not to get mad like Mama does.

Payday is on the fifteenth and then you can call me where I can talk to you on the phone instead of in these letters that you don't answer. Mama's probably not giving them to you, seeing that she thinks I'm unfit and all.

I get six dollars an hour, which is pretty good considering most jailbirds can't hardly find a job in this town, so I can afford it. For your birthday I'll send you one of those prepaid phones and you can call me anytime you want. I'll make sure to keep my cell charged all the time.

Delores, Pablo, and Annie are hollering for me to hurry up because it's time to go to their church. Yippee. This custody lawyer I talked to today says it'll help if I'm trying to be a productive member of the community. Best thing about him is that he takes payments.

Well, Annie's stomping up the stairs so I'd better go.

REMEMBER THE LADY who smiled at me in the lunchroom on my first day? She goes to Delores and them's church. Her name is Zara and she's from Russia. Her two little girls are younger than you. One's in fifth grade and one's in seventh. Both on the honor roll. Can you imagine? Zara goes home after work and spends all night helping her two girls with their homework and she can't hardly speak English. Back in Russia, she was a school teacher but now she makes minimum wage fixing old slot machines. Get this—she don't even mind that she's being paid only what the government makes them pay—she says her girls can be something when they're grown.

I felt bad because of how mean I was to you about the Earth's crust, being I can't even remember the other parts myself except something about a hot molten center. I've made up my mind to set a little money aside for your college fund every payday. You can be anything that you want. Please pick something important, like a lawyer or a congresswoman. Even if you don't ever call me, that money will still be here waiting for you when you get ready for it.

REMEMBER WHEN PAUL WOULD HAVE PARTIES at our house and I'd be waiting downstairs while the guests arrived? How all those women would walk in our fancy house and look at me as if they'd like to tear my designer dresses right off? Paul never did let me say much but it didn't matter. Women wanted to be me.

I miss being someone to be jealous of.

Today was bill-paying day at work and I had to enter all these invoices into the computer then print out the checks. Bet I wasted half a box. How was I supposed to know that the printer sucked the checks in backwards if nobody told me? When Alice let me off of work I went to the library—where Annie works part time—and asked if there was anything about QuickBooks. She helped me find one but it's pretty old. Annie said how much can bill paying change? I read until suppertime and the book didn't say nothing about how to put checks into the printer. What am I gonna do?

Delores said she'd be praying for me. I wanted to say thanks a lot for nothing. I don't need no prayers, I need to be able to do what I'm supposed to do with nobody yelling at me about how stupid I am.

TODAY, I SENT YOU A TEN DOLLAR CARD to add to the TracFone minutes. I don't have any way of knowing when you're running short but thought they might come in handy since I know how strict Mama can be. She won't ever let you talk on the phone with anybody who's any fun. Especially if that someone is me. Last time I called, she told me to stop calling you, that I was never going to get you back, and that I deserved to go straight to hell. ~~Fuck~~ Forget her.

At lunch today I went to the Dollar Store with Zara and she bought her girls two outfits each. Remember when I used to take you shopping and we'd buy anything we wanted on Paul's credit card? What I'd give to be able to buy you clothes, even cheap three dollar ones. As it is, most of my paycheck is going into this jar I have on top of my dresser. It's for your education so you won't ever have to depend on a man to make you feel important.

Delores and Annie say that what Jesus did is what makes them important, but they've never done time because of what a man did to them. Like a man can make their lives better, or something. I've never had a man do anything but ~~fuck up~~ mess up mine.

Wonder if Pablo can tattoo something to that effect on my leg?

Or maybe on my butt?

Yeah, on my butt.

Maybe big red lip prints.

I'VE FIGURED OUT WHAT TO DO with the checks in the printer. Before I stuck them in, I Xeroxed the checks to see if they'd come out the right way and they did. So when the program asked me if they were printed correctly I clicked NO and put the real checks in. Is your mother a ~~fucking~~ genius or what?

Zara had to work through lunch because she didn't make production so I read another of Annie's novels. This one was about this ~~whore~~ lady who married a farmer but she kept wanting to return to her old life but he kept loving her so much he'd drag her back to their farm. (Paul sure isn't dragging me back, is he? He's probably got some other stupid bimbo to deliver his drugs for him. I wonder what he's telling her they are? He told me they were Astros tickets.)

After I'd finished my sandwich, my boss told me to come to the office even though I still had ten minutes left because the mail came and she wanted me to balance the bank statement so that her accountant could make some kind of report for a renewal of the bank loan. I told her the bank statement was already balanced, because I know that checkbook's right because I don't trust the computer and it has the same number that I do on my green ledger. She got all snotty and told me to print out the computer report. So I did, but she said it wasn't right. Why couldn't she have told me about this bank statement ~~shit~~ business a month ago?

Two hours later I was still trying to figure out why the checking account didn't say what the bank said it should. Alice glared at me the whole time. I told her that the last bookkeeper must have been stealing from them because they didn't never have that much money—nothing matched on any day according to that bank. She got all mad at me like I couldn't add and subtract. The longer I spent on it, the hotter she got. Then she just lost it and said that the check register balance wasn't supposed to match the statement and I didn't know nothing about bank reconciliations. And I told her that she was ~~damn~~ right because drug dealers didn't have bank accounts. She said it was too bad my brain wasn't as big as my boobs and that if I couldn't figure it out by Friday I was fired.

If I lose my job how are we going to be together again? How am I supposed to do this in four days when I've never done anything like this before?

I just don't know.

Tonight when that guy at church asks if anyone needs prayer, I'm going to tell them flat out what I need help on. ~~Fuck~~ Forget all that *unspoken* business. If they want to think I'm dumb, they can.

I don't care anymore.

A#NOTHER FRUSTRATING DAY# trying to reconcile that ~~damn~~ bank statement. When I came home, Annie and Pablo were in the kitchen making tamales for some kind of fundraiser deal. I wanted to help but Annie shook her head. She said I had wrinkles in my forehead and she'd brought me a surprise and to go read chapter three.

In her black bag I found a beginning accounting book, heavy as all get out. I trudged upstairs feeling hopeless, pretty much the opposite of what Annie was hoping (I could tell by her frown). My whole life is out of balance. Like a book is gonna help.

Deposits in transit, outstanding checks, adjusting journal entries—why can't they just use plain English? It took me two hours just to memorize the definitions so I could keep everything straight.

Deposits in transit—money you think you have because it's in the checkbook but the bank doesn't know yet.

Outstanding checks—money long gone but the bank hasn't caught wind of it yet.

Adjusting journal entries—the bank knows you were either totally in the dark or you've really ~~fucked~~ messed up.

The chapter review problems were easy. According to the back of the book, my even-numbered ones were right. Don't know about the odd ones because there was only even-numbered answers. When I finished studying, I felt real good about work tomorrow and wished it were already time to go, but then I saw where you'd left a voicemail and it was too late to call you back. It was great hearing your voice.

Even if you did say that you hated my guts and for me to leave you alone.

F#OR THE PAST TWO DAYS# I've been using a highlighter to mark off the stuff that matches on the bank statement and the check register, then trying to figure out what to do with all this ~~shit~~ stuff that's left over. The bank has all kinds of transactions I don't have and I've got deposits and checks that should've cleared already. What do I do to fix it? Alice kept looking over my shoulder and ~~damn near~~ hyperventilating. Then the accountant called to see where we were at because he's got to have the numbers first thing in the morning (and not last thing, like I'd been counting on.)

At lunch I went out to the smoking area to cry. The lizards kept me company. This time the big one bit the little one's neck and locked his legs through hers. No question on what was going on there. The little lizard's eyes never left mine, her mouth gaped open like she was screaming. I reached out and grabbed her, to save her, but her tail broke off in my hand. I screamed and dropped it where it wriggled on the concrete while she scurried away.

Zara brought me a tissue and a turkey sandwich, staying with me for a while. She rubbed my shoulder and said that our boss was no good because she only hired people who couldn't get any other job.

I cried harder. She's right, Mama's right, and you're right. I'm dumb and I deserve to get fired. There's not any other jobs for me, not any good ones with my record. Paul always told me how smart I was. That should've been my first clue. I can't even help a stupid lizard.

Zara said I didn't break off the lizard's tail—that she broke it off herself as a defense thing. Must've read it in one of her kids' books. But I still felt bad.

When I got back to my desk Alice handed me my last paycheck and then the owner watched me pack up your pictures. As he was walking me toward the front door I couldn't stop thinking about that little lizard. I couldn't leave her. So I made up a story about my cigarette lighter was out back and he let me go. She was long gone, but I found her tail where I dropped it. The stump wasn't bloody or slimy, so I just slipped it into my pocket.

Then the owner wouldn't let me go back inside to say goodbye to Zara, because he said I might sabotage their computer system—like I'd even want to do that. People just want to believe the worst. When we got around the corner of the building, he pressed me up against the brick wall. I just froze. He ran his hands all over me and said if I was real nice to him, maybe he could work something out with Alice.

I still wanted my job, but not that way. So my knee told him no thanks.

What Alice and the pervert didn't know was I have copies of everything at home. She said I had until eight o'clock tomorrow morning to get that reconciliation done so I'm going to hold her to that. I might not be smart but I can learn. I've been working on it all night now. There's only one thing I can't figure out—why the reconciled balance doesn't match what's on the books.

I've done all I can do.

THE ACCOUNTANT DRIVES A BLACK LEXUS just like my old one. The only reason I know that is because his secretary said he wasn't in yet, so I waited for him in their parking lot. When he finally pulled up, I introduced myself and gave him the bank reconciliation. He must have thought I was a lunatic—stalking him like I did—so I explained how I was fired yesterday and how I needed my job to get you back. He rolled his eyes and said for me to come with him into his office.

At his desk, he glanced over my paperwork and his face relaxed. He said I'd done a pretty good job, like he was surprised. I asked how I could've done that because my balance didn't match the books. He said he'd made an adjustment in prior years that their old bookkeeper had never imported. Whatever that meant.

He asked me what I thought the hardest part was. Duh—trying to figure out who messed up and how to fix it. He said to keep in mind the reconciliation wasn't about who was right or wrong but working out the discrepancies.

In a weird way, that made sense. I thought about you and Mama, Paul, and even Alice—

how we had all this stuff still between us that I don't know how to make right.

The accountant said seeing that I didn't have a job how would I like to come to work for him?

I told him the truth—that I'd been in jail and how you didn't even want to see me anymore and how I didn't know anything about keeping books and I wasn't gonna sleep with him, no matter how much he paid me. He said he didn't want to sleep with me and that I knew more about books than I realized and he'd teach me more if I were willing to learn. And I believed him, because his eyes never once'd moved below my neck.

He held out his hand to me and I took it, just like a real businesswoman.

I said fine, I'd start tomorrow.

But he said no, I'd start right now.

Most of the day I had no idea what I was doing, but it was different than feeling stupid. I was scared and excited all at the same time. Somehow I knew that I'd catch on eventually. After work, I was flat worn out. As I crossed over the railroad track between our office and the café next door, I saw a patch of dandelions. Why is it that the dead white ones seem more alive than the living yellow ones? I pulled the lizard's tail from my pocket and buried it there in the blooms. Then I picked a white stem and blew the fuzzies into a wish for you and me.

AND WHY THEOLOGY SCOTT CAIRNS

because the first must be first
　—Milosz

And the first, if you don't mind my saying, is both an uttered
notion of the truth and a provisional, even giddy apprehension
of its reach. The day—quite fortunately, a winter's day—is censed
with wood smoke, and the wood smoke is remarkably, is richly
spiced with evergreen; you can almost taste the resin.

Or, I can. Who knows what you're up to? The day itself
is shrouded, wrapped, or tucked, say, within a veil of wood smoke
and low cloud, and decidedly gray, but lined as well with intermittent,
slanted rays of startlingly brilliant, impossibly white light—just here,
and over there, and they move a bit, shifting round as high weather

shoves the clouds about. Theology is a distinctly rare, a puzzling
study, given that its practitioners are happiest when the terms
of their discovery fall well short of their projected point; this
is where they likely glimpse their proof. Rare as well
is the theologian's primary stipulation that all that is explicable

is somewhat less than interesting. In any case, the day
keeps loping right along, and blurs into the night, which itself
will fairly likely press into another clouded day, et cetera.
The future isn't written, isn't fixed, and the proof of that is how
sure we are—if modestly—that every moment matters.

Take this one. We stand before another day extending like
a scarf of cloud, or wood smoke, or incense reaching past what's visible.
And sure, you could rush ahead, abandoning what lies in reach in favor
of what isn't—but you don't, and the others at your side are pleased
to have you with them, supposing that we'll make our way together.

LAMENT IN A COUNTRY GRAVEYARD MARIANNE TAYLOR

Blessings turned to blasphemies,
Holy deeds to despites.
          —Anon., 15th century

Beyond wood's edge, we bury our friend,
and where we stand the sun illuminates
no just cause, only fields fertilized
yet unsown. Another contradiction.

> *Prepare the ground to bear the seed*
> *spray nitric acids on dark tilled soil*
> *bless with anhydrous ammonia*
> *(by the tankful) the fruit to come.*

> > No warning thunder, the hailstorm battered
> > his fit body, flung toxic rings around wide eyes
> > flushed out color, furrowed firm skin.
> > Put a neon question in his mouth.

> > And left us dumb. When a verdict's so loud,
> > words vaporize, compassion dissolves.
> > All to do was bear witness,
> > ride it out. Exhausted. Still intact.

Holy water, bless this grave, quench
his thirst, our thirst. Wash away
our sins, and bring us peace that defies
gravity, drifts with the afternoon.

LAMENT IN A COUNTRY GRAVEYARD

Here is no breeze, no stirring at all
just our awkward tableau, blankly lit
by a sun edging its way across a
hollow sky, cobalt blue.

Tonight, perhaps, dark clouds
will up-end our leftover moon.
A wayward wind will rant, sweep off
ill death, sow seeds in safer fields.

MISS SWEETY'S ROCK-OLA MACHINE J. MARCUS WEEKLEY

NOBODY WOULD TOUCH IT and the thing would start playing whatever tune it had on its mechanical mind. New people would shove a quarter or two in the slot and start punching away at the little yellow buttons and when nothing would come out, they'd curse and holler and demand to get their money back.

Miss Sweety didn't say anything and pointed to the sign she wrote herself, the one taped over the rock-ola—"Don't expect to get your quarter back. This masheen got a mind of its own." She was smarty like that. Then she went to wiping out glasses or sometimes sit there and smoke while that newbody argued some more till eventually they gave up and played pool or bought a drink or walked out.

Right about then that crazy thing would start singing—its favorite was Beach Boys—and for a while, Miss Sweety hated them boys until after a while she just got used to it I guess.

Well, one day I was down helping Miss Sweety because we knew each other since I was a little girl. I usually swept and cleaned tables. I moved all the chairs over to the wall, then the tables, and sometime in the middle the rock-ola would start up and a couple people would come in once it started, maybe before. You could hear it all the way over from Finley. I swear it played for an hour at a time and wouldn't shut up and I don't know why Miss Sweety wouldn't take out the plug. It helped me work faster or she liked it I guess.

So, I was sweeping and Miss Sweety stood behind the counter wiping out glasses and her silverware with a white rag. Barnabus had come in, and his nephew Steve, and they were sitting next to the front door, out of my way. Steve sipped on a root beer, Barnabus a beer. Barnabus was always watching me like he was hungry, but I knew about that, so I swept and didn't look up much. And he was married anyway.

That silly machine started up again, only it was something like a preacher coming out of it, a booming preacher's voice talking about Barnabus. Scared Sweety so much she dropped a glass and I dropped the broom and we both stood there staring at the machine squatted against the far wall.

"Barnabus Gretchum, you need to confess. You've been looking in rooms you have no business in and you've been searching for a fountain that ain't yours to drink in."

I checked over in Barnabus' direction and he sat there like he was hearing directly from God. Miss Sweety wasn't stopping it. I started blushing. Was that voice talking about me?

"You need to confess to your wife and you need to confess to your children and you need to drink from your own fountain, to sleep in the rooms that I've already given you."

Miss Sweety still stood behind the counter, but Steve looked at his uncle like the man had been caught smoking marijuana cigarettes behind the church. I wanted the voice to shut up. It might start talking about me any minute.

"And Steven Green, you need to deny yourself. Stop taking liberties with your mama's purse and stop taking liberties with your mind and stop all that nonsense about doing nothing with yourself. You're worth more than that foolishness and there ain't no need for it. You got good people who love you, who support you."

Steve spilled his root beer. It ran over the table to his lap but he didn't get up. He stared at the rock-ola and nodded, mouth open like a bread sack.

Miss Sweety headed toward the machine, looking fairly nervous herself. Maybe she didn't want to hear nothing neither.

"And you, Sweety Thornton—"

She unplugged the rusty rock-ola and it shut up. Nobody said a word.

Miss Sweety's was hot now, like all the air stopped moving, though the door and windows were open. And it only being March.

"Don't try to silence me, woman."

Miss Sweety screamed and covered her ears and crumpled on the floor, started crying.

The machine sat quiet for a second, its insides whirring. Everybody didn't say a thing.

"Sweety Thornton, you have been a faithful servant, a true friend, a sister and a mother to those who weren't your own. Well done."

She cried louder then, saying, "Thank you, thank you," and looked up at the machine like it was Jesus His self. I thought maybe there could be a good word for me.

"But Sister, be warned—the first of next month you will meet me at the gates."

Miss Sweety? My heart got going faster and faster.

The rock-ola was quiet. Not even a whir. Miss Sweety cried quietly on the floor and Barnabus ran out the front door. Steve stayed in his seat. I waited. Sweat went down my back and my hands started shaking. What was my word?

Not a sound.

I stood staring at that rock-ola for a little while, then hurried and plugged it back in, hoping for something. After a while it went ahead and played "Fun, fun, fun" and I kicked that stupid machine harder than I ever kicked anything in my life.

I never went back to Miss Sweety's after. Lots of people didn't believe us. But sure enough, she died on the first of April, April Fool's, but I didn't laugh at that. I didn't go to the funeral. I didn't cry. I didn't cry when Barnabus' wife left him or when Steve got his scholarship to some university over in Alabama. I wanted to know why God spoke to those other three folks through a dumb rock-ola machine and hadn't saw fit to speak to me. I ain't going to speak to Him or anybody else until I hear my word. I didn't and I haven't.

FEAST DAY OF ST. URSULA DEBRA KAUFMAN

She was a nun in a former life, said the husband
at a table full of friends. His friends

and their wives. A quick embarrassed laugh
as she sat there gripping her cup of tea.

That she didn't storm out or throw the cup
only showed how right he was,

how nice she was. *Nice*, from Latin
nescius—ignorant, not to know.

But isn't that what he liked about her
when they met—how she walked alone,

like a child or saint, through the woods
without binoculars or notepad?

When they'd known each other just a few months,
he'd stroked her throat and she'd said,

If I was a cat I'd purr, though minutes later
she was ready to be on her own again.

The friends are leaving: *thank you, good night*.
She follows them out. A dog barks, then another.

Forgive us our trespasses.
At the end of the street a field opens

to the sky—Hercules, Pegasus,
Cassiopeia. In the billions of stars

she sees pairs, opposites.
A person could pray here if she could think how.

EASTER DEBRA KAUFMAN

The day was chilly and wet
and I wanted it
to swallow me whole,
absorb me into
the myriad droplets of mist.
It wasn't death I yearned for
but return as something
other than human—
jonquil, goldfinch, vixen, snake.
It's the weariness of being conscious,
of being in the body—its demands
of feed me, stretch me, let me rest.
Not to compare myself to the Christ, mind,
but don't we all sometimes feel
we carry that weight?
You may believe in a savior
and others fancy themselves as such,
but I want to believe in something smaller
and possible: the good hearts and common sense
of most of us; that we will do what's right
in time; that our bodies, our blood,
will transubstantiate into earth, air, water.
The world, without end. Amen.

APRIL FOOLS DEBRA KAUFMAN

Grackles have taken
over the feeder. Nasty things,
with their cold white eyes
and oily heads. Titmice
watch from the dogwoods;
doves mourn on the lawn.

There's a deep-down fatigue
I'm longing to shake.
When the sun comes out
and the downy woodpeckers return—
fresh suet is all it takes—
I decide today must be a reprieve,
ending a month of gloomy weather,
bad decisions, small collisions.

The challenge: how not to see
everything now through a pall
shrouding our poor earth.
This earth that holds us here
despite the daily assaults
from those who bully their way in,
those who wait too patiently too long,
those who survive with the clearest
eye for vengeance.

What can we do—
sing the songs our parents taught us?
Or, like that mockingbird
tilting on the high wire,
can we mix up the scraps
and scoldings of others
to sing the gospel of a new world?

GRACE DEBRA KAUFMAN

Grace is gangly,
a tall drink of water;
her countenance is pleasing.

Her place in the arbor
scented with ripe muscadine.
Sun filters through
the lace of mimosa leaves.

She carries a tray
of refreshments for us.
No one notices
how perfect it all is

until she trips, spilling
the drinks. Glass shatters
at our feet, and we see

reflected in each shard
the light that makes
all this possible—
the beauty, the fall,

the sweeping up
after.

DANCES WITH OLIVIA ALYS MATTHEWS

I CAST A SIDELONG GLANCE at her profile as she sits in the rickety brown chair next to me—her eyes blank, her face riveted. She is not used to this place. The gleeful, amateur artistry on the walls, the dirty basement floor, the well-dressed and made-up figurines that fiddle with their fingernails as the message drones monotonously on from the aged lips of the man at the head of the table—it's all so alien to her; I can feel it as undoubtedly as the impatient tapping of my foot against the cold, hard floor. I know that she thinks she does not belong here. I look at her almost startlingly white face, the palest in the room; her large, enveloping brown eyes, arched by sharp, dark brows; her skinny little legs; her electric pinkish-red hair. How mundane the rest of us must look in comparison to the utter shock of her features in this place.

We don't wear the same shoe size, so she couldn't borrow my dainty gold ballet flats like we had planned. She had to wear what she brought—her three-pound-each black boots with flames inching up the sides, pentagrams on the toes. I told her not to worry, nobody looked at feet. I guess it was kind of a lie.

On my other side, my friends are whispering and giggling, writing notes and applying makeup, which I am accustomed to. The teacher doesn't seem to notice.

"So Jesus came to Mary and Martha's house, where they were mourning Lazarus' death. When he arrived, Mary said—can anybody tell me what Mary said to Jesus? It's John, chapter eleven, I believe."

Olivia glances at the open Bible on her lap, as though surprised it hasn't burned her yet. And then she speaks—bravely, confidently, but so, so softly— "I believe You are the Messiah."

I have known her for about five years now, and I have always admired her versatility, that ability to make the best of any situation. Wherever she goes, she does not try to fit in but she always tries to contribute.

I am proud of her.

"If You had been here, Lazarus wouldn't have died," Chelsea paraphrases from across the room, solemn and pretty. Church-pretty.

"Exactly," pronounces the teacher with a warm,

withered smile. "Good job. Mary said that if Jesus . . ." And he goes off again on some tangent that I am not listening to, because I am looking at Olivia and Olivia has looked down.

Her hands are folded, the way they never are, and her eyes are wide and unseeing as she stares at the slate-blue floor. I feel a pang of guilt at her sadness and her smallness in this room. I never should have brought her. Olivia should never look this lost.

Last night on a crowded dance floor her eyes were there, where we were, creasing and smiling. You could see her purple-and-red braces because she laughed. Her skin was the same shade as it is now, but it was not ghostly; it was lovely, like if you put powder on a tiny china doll and flickered all those multi-colored dance lights over it. There, she walked around and her long red dress and her cranberry hair and her crazy black heels and the temporary Chinese tattoo on her back attracted compliments and smiles and friendly recognition.

Here, they attract stares.

Last night she took my hands in hers and we spun and swung around like fools, her leading me because she dances like a dream and I can't dance to save my life. It was like chaos, like freedom, like the wild motion of sisterhood and all the love that latches us the way our hands latch and cling. Olivia is complex and amazing. She is whirling and shaking and rolling and radiating *life*.

I bite my lip in the stillness. Her hair is throwing color against the white. Her eyes are tired.

"Are you okay?" I murmur finally.

She lifts her head and slightly raises her eyebrows at me. With her eyes still empty, she nods. Looks away.

Then, suddenly—and for just a moment—my empathy is so acute that I swear I become her. And out of nowhere I can see God. So clearly.

This is who God is. God is a white wall and a cement floor and a Jesus-loves-me Sunday school lesson. God is the stone-faced redneck boy and the giggly, pretty girl who couldn't care less that Jesus cares. God is the man who does not answer my questions, who ignores my attempts; the woman who judges the very *nerve* of me to be myself; the ones who whisper about me from a safe distance and wonder why I am here until it's time for me to walk again, unaffected, away from it all. God is whatever the hell they want Him to be. God is a lie.

So one more walks away from the building all stained with white, and she will never walk in again. One more returns to her true friends later that evening in total relief, her clothes skewered, her body relaxed and at home, her eyes again vivid, and she laughs to them about what she learned in church that morning with those crazy little Christians. And they laugh with her, because it's never made sense to them, either. The only reality is love—beautiful, all-conquering love—which, judging from their brief tastes of the *wonders* and the *salvation* of Jesus Christ, He most definitely is not.

One more walks away, but it does not matter. How could it? Christians are all the same. Jesus loves them, this they know; for their Bible tells them so. But Jesus does not love Olivia, because she is different and because she is Olivia.

I would like to think that God would be like me, and recognize her better on the dance floor. I would like to think that if He were here now, she would be the first to feel the warmth of His touch on her hands, as real and as accepting as my own.

WE THE PEOPLE OF BARBIE RENEE RONIKA KLUG

The most terrifying thing is to accept oneself completely.
—Carl Jung

THE BRICKS LOOSENED OVER THE YEARS as our fathers lifted us above the fence into each other's backyard. We were both Indian—not the kind that lived on nearby reservations—and Rani was a year older than I. By the time she entered kindergarten, we were introducing ourselves as cousins. People didn't question how one cousin could be Hindu while the other was Sikh, or that Rani's mom was a Brahmin while my mother was Irish-Polish.

On Friday or Saturday nights for most of the weekends of our childhood, Rani and I slept over at each other's houses. Together, we discovered our fear of the Wicked Witch of the West, our understanding that books were to be cherished, and our affection for the stick figured, bellybutton-less blondes in their Dream House behind my bedroom door. By the time I was in fourth grade, the dolls had become Rockers, owners of a convertible, and were caregivers to an oversized poodle in a beret named Prince.

Barbie Millicent Roberts has been welcomed into homes like Rani's and mine for decades; every second, three of her namesake dolls are sold around the world. She has a bestselling children's computer software line, and a top-rated girls' website, *Barbie.com*, where eight million monthly users spend an average of forty-two minutes per visit and read her stated online mission: to engage, enchant and empower girls by inspiring them to be creative and explore their individual interests. Barbie is a high achiever and expects nothing less of her community of girls.

Barbie is international by birth. Her creator, Ruth Handler, noticed her daughter Barbara preferred dressing adult paper dolls to playing mommy to baby dolls. Handler suggested a Barbie prototype to her husband Elliot, a co-founder of the Mattel toy industry. Her husband and the board of directors at Mattel derided the idea, assuming the doll unmarketable. Ruth Handler was vacationing in Germany sometime later when she noticed Lilli, a doll that resembled the idea she initially had in mind. Lilli originally was advertised to adult men in bars and tobacco shops as a "society girl" who "knew what she wanted and wasn't above using men to get it." Young German girls began to favor the dolls because they could dress them up in separately sold outfits. Handler bought three dolls, giving one to her daughter and taking two to Mattel, which bought the rights to Lilli, redesigned the doll, and introduced her to the public at the New York International American Toy Fair on what is now her official birthday, March 9, 1959.[1]

According to Mattel, Barbie's career began as a fashion model before she entered college. Since her freshman days, she has—among eighty other feats—traveled internationally, competed as an Olympic swimmer, worked as a paleontologist, voyaged space, and served in the armed forces (with a Pentagon approved wardrobe). Through the White House Project, the non-partisan organization behind the fictional Party of Girls!, Barbie campaigned twice for the US presidency so girls could "think about turning Barbie's Dream House into the White House." She lost both times to George W. Bush. In her endeavors, Barbie has championed causes to educate girls, to protect animals, and to diversify and unite communities, all while wearing one of over a billion pairs of shoes or a couture outfit from Gucci, Dolce & Gabbana, or Versace, all in signature Barbie pink. By 2002, she had starred in two films—first in the *Nutcracker* and then in the title role of *Rapunzel*. On February 12, 2004, CNN reported Barbie and Ken were separating but would "remain friends." Barbie felt she needed to have some "quality time apart" from her husband of forty-three years. Barbie rebounded with a new boyfriend, Blaine, an Australian surfer who lives on the West Coast for his "Cali Guy" line, who has suntanned skin, complementing the newest brown-sugared Barbie look. Barbie's foray into new territory was short-lived; in 2006, Mattel announced that Ken and Barbie had reunited.

But Barbie's accomplishments go unnoticed by the average consumer. With a ubiquitous stereotype as the gorgeous-blonde-with-a-tiny-waist-that-could-never-hold-up-those-enormous-boobs, Barbie's reception hasn't been as a reflection of feminine progress, but as a sexual reminder of feminine frustration; if Barbie is the standard for how women should look, then based on hair color alone most women have failed. Needless to say, when observers examine beyond the plastic, they might discover a doll representative of a massive, diverse populace that influences her decisions and appearance. Barbie exhibits a changing society in her comprehensive résumé, her expanding circle of ethnic friends, her recently redistributed-to-reflect-reality proportions, even in her option out of marriage and selection of a younger man. Still, the public and her supporters agree Barbie can be held accountable for the choices girls make and for the insecurities they have: "Barbie is often looked upon as an icon of Western childhood. Her popularity ensures that her effect on the play of Western children attracts a high degree of scrutiny. The criticisms leveled at her are often based around the idea of children considering Barbie a role model and attempting to emulate her."[2]

DURING THE 1980S IN PHOENIX, where Rani and I played, we knew we would go to college, but our decision was not based on Barbie as a role model. Our parents were educated, and our fathers' steadfast similarity was that their children would know the value of a work ethic—personally, academically, and professionally. Rani was the quiet-type who could articulate herself well around adults. I spent afternoons writing stories in sequined notebooks or teaching Judy Blume books to Barbie, bears, and Cabbage Patch Kids seated attentively on the carpet. Our preternatural maturity shone during playtime. We pierced Barbie's ears with our cubic zirconium birthstone earrings—rubies for Rani's, sapphires for mine. Barbie's makers hadn't updated her look since the seventies, so we cut bangs for her. Sometimes there would be mousse. We mixed and matched wardrobes. At once, we became fashion designers, actresses, wives, mothers, creators.

In all my time with Barbie, I never considered my hair color inferior because Barbie's was blonde. I did, however, excitedly reach out for the dark-haired dolls not because I was in search of validation, but because they looked like me. When Barbie was undressed, I acknowledged that one day, like Barbie, I too would have breasts. Somehow, because of the years we have spent dressing and undressing Barbie, she has become the reason women develop dysfunction or choose peculiar lifestyle—even religious—choices. With political correctness serving as the dictator of how and with what children should play, there are numerous controversies surrounding the eventual ramifications girls will encounter for playing with the disproportionate tow-headed dolls.

In a December 2005 report, psychologists at Bath University in England indicated that girls maim their Barbies in a variety of ways, such as decapitating or microwaving them. Dr. Agnes Nairn states, "When we asked groups of junior school children about Barbie, the doll provoked rejection, hatred, and violence," while, she suggests, older girls rebuff Barbie dolls because they negatively remind them of their often alienated and insufferable childhoods.[3]

When Mattel released "Teen Talk Barbie" in the early nineties, the Barbie Liberation Organization (BLO)—comprised of parents, feminists and other activists—purchased hundreds of Barbie and GI Joe dolls and modified their voice circuitry. Instead of the now-classic Barbie catch phrases, "Math is tough!" (which, for many, it is) and "Wanna have a pizza party?" (which, for many, sounds like fun) the dolls retort, "Eat lead, Cobra!" and "Dead men tell no lies," the latter clearly offering sound advice and fairly representing seven-year-old girls.[4]

American conservatives—secular or Christian—oftentimes protest against Mattel's marketing of an increasingly liberal Barbie. Perhaps they fear the doll's acceptance of societal shifts will solidify a place for questionable lifestyle choices, like divorce or fornication.

The same sentiment is evident overseas, where many traditional communities disapprove of permissive Western thinking. Saudi Arabian anti-Semites forbid children from playing with Barbie because creator Ruth Handler was Jewish.[5] Middle Eastern Islamic groups have boycotted the promiscuous Western Barbie for "revealing clothes and shameful postures." In response, they have replaced her with Fulla, a doll with dark eyes, dark hair, less makeup and a fuller, sportier figure. Fulla, according to her designer, is more "modest" than Barbie, with "Muslim values," her own pink felt prayer rug, and a *hijab*—the traditional Islamic outdoor head covering. Now the Muslim world's best-selling doll, Fulla markets her own line of clothing, breakfast cereal, cutlery and bicycles—all in trademark "Fulla pink."6

Evidently, the emphasis in America—and in many countries abroad—is on the values a doll can uphold for a nation, a culture, and not on the whimsy she may provide a girl who wants to remain just this—a girl.

Well before archetypes of beauty are foisted to them by the media, most people realize that young girls cause plenty of verbal and emotional damage to their classmates without Barbie's influence. When a little girl is refused friendship on the playground for an apparent genetic defect or mismatched socks, the ensuing alienation from that rejection far outweighs any projected confusion a girl may receive from playing with a tall, white Barbie doll. To blame Barbie is equitable. To blame ourselves is unthinkable. In an advanced culture of lofty, progressive ideas, why should we bear the burden of the fact that we have cast our daughters to swine by not teaching them to be kind to others, regardless of race, wealth, appearance, or intellect? The mutilation of a Barbie doll perhaps has less to do with Barbie than with the angst of childhood.

In the mature world of an educated, attractive female, what Barbie has done with her life is enviable, and perhaps impossible. According to *PBS.com*,

> After a newspaper reported Alicia Booth's nomination as sexiest woman in Charlotte, she was removed from the anchor desk and demoted to reporter. Though the decision may seem unfair, it was apparently based on focus group research that suggested Booth was "too attractive" to appeal to female viewers. In short, Booth's looks got in the way.7

Our minds vex us; the thoughts we allow to estrange others, and ourselves, from one another in a distorted way form a community of universality: we are insecure as women.

THE FIRST AND ONLY TIME I was stung by a desert insect was in Rani's backyard. My dad had just passed me over the fence, where Rani's dad helped me slide down the wall. Afterwards, I stood talking or daydreaming—I can't remember which, as they both came naturally and frequently to me—and reached back to scratch my neck. The cause of the itch, a resting wasp, pricked my left pinky and made me cry. So much made me cry as a kid but usually my cries were silent, betrayed only by the tearing up of my eyes, the failed stoicism of my chin. The wasp sent me howling into the house, where Rani's mother tended to the pain.

The first and only time I stole was from Rani's bedroom. I still don't know what compelled me, a do-gooder, straight-A, teacher's pet, to swipe the miniature metal flashlight from under Rani's pillow. About a year later, Rani found the flashlight at my house and told me she had one just like it. If I had that flashlight today, I would track down Rani's address and mail it to her, with a note asking her forgiveness.

I once went shopping with Rani and her friend, who was also older than me. I didn't know what to do with myself around sophisticated girls. This was my first shopping trip without my mom. I picked up different items and affirmed, or praised, anything they showed me. But I didn't really have an opinion. Everything was "cute." I didn't want to disagree with the popular opinion.

The following week, the eighth grade journalism crew handed out awards to us seventh graders. Rani handed me the "How Cute" award—because it was my favorite phrase. It seemed that my personality, or lack thereof, had not been reduced but embodied by capturing—now on parchment—how afraid I was to be myself. I spent nights thereafter editing out that phrase from my vernacular, and on subsequent trips to the mall I made certain I noted nothing cute about any item.

One of the last nights I remember Rani staying over, I pulled out the familiar suitcase of Barbie clothes, and handed Rani the Peaches-N-Cream doll she favored. Rani lowered the doll to her lap and stated she did not want to play Barbie anymore. "It's boring. This is kid stuff."

I couldn't argue with her; it wasn't my nature. I put the clothes and dolls away and, after that, took them out only when I knew no one was looking. Later on, when I was much too old to play with dolls, I found myself reaching into the attic for the box where my mom had helped me wrap and store my Barbie dolls. I tried to play with them, sometimes dressed them, but I could not capture the feeling—that freedom—I clung to when I was younger. From then on, my escape was in books, in movies, in music, in being alone with imagination—others' or my own—to cry over, sing to, twirl to, or to repeat in my personal dialogue.

But I never really put Barbie away.

Twenty-three years since kindergarten, even after several declinations, I am in pursuit of a doctorate in English Literature. I am a college instructor of composition and creative writing. Rani is a lawyer. She got married about three years ago, but I was in Europe during the wedding and couldn't make it to California, where she still lives. I returned to my then-home on Long Island, where I stored the invitation—on red paisley embroidered soft paper—and wondered what kind of lawyer, what kind of wife, Rani was. I was certain her time at Pepperdine created in her an appreciation for beauty, for wealth, for scholarship.

The last time I saw her was when I visited her in Malibu during her freshman year. We ate dinner overlooking the Pacific, and Rani commented on the attitudes of Pepperdine students, not hiding her disparagement of their complacent, self-obsessed attitudes. When it was my turn to decide my future college, I too chose California, a school that had once been offered at Pepperdine's current campus, but instead selected the pocket community of La Mirada, a university hidden away in a halcyon neighborhood. Based on Rani's warning, I wasn't ready to face the possible judgment of Pepperdine's post-pubescent, erudite crowd. My selection of a university whose prerequisite was that all students adhere to Christian doctrine and principles was a survival tool. If I were going to face the world alone, at least I'd ensure it was a kind world.

In the ten years since I have seen Rani, our paths have led to different cities, schools, majors, and loves. She was a speechwriter for Kofi Annan. I worked alongside Amy Tan and Dianne Wiest. We've both seen cultures and climates that singularize the salsa and cacti of igneous Arizona. We have chosen cities that would advance us, lead us to our truer selves. She found love somewhere in Chicago. I am still searching for love, somewhere in Tempe, where I now reside, where I have returned after ten years of pursuing greener grass. In revisiting this landscape, I revisit youth. I revisit a predominantly white-bred childhood, where Rani and I stuck to each other because we were peculiarly colored, featured, and parented. Kids on the playground called me nigger. They made fun of my Indian nose. My Indian food.

My Indian father's accent. They called me Gandhi.

I am guilty of second-guessing myself. My relationship with and comparisons to Rani are my proof. All these years, my insecurity has grown in my need to develop a flexibility, to mold my opinion to others' expectations, to be nice, to be liked, to be perfect. Barbie is just the decoy. If we can continue looking outside ourselves to remedy what aches within, then the pain will only be pacified, not healed. In a nation of provocative beauty, expendable wealth, and half-lit glass ceilings, women can only run so far and so fast before they collapse onto a pavement of recognition: *this is not working.*

I forgive myself for the "how cutes" of my childhood; the mismatched socks; the ugly facial features; the funny accents; the girls on the playground who wouldn't play. I forgive myself of the rejections of my adulthood: the scholastic disappointments; the financial anxieties; the absence of eloquence around celebrities and mentors; the abandonment of relationships. I need to call up Rani not to find out what, but how, she is doing. I need to learn that just because society focuses on Barbie's beauty doesn't mean Barbie has to, and she doesn't. Although she maintains herself and her wardrobe, Barbie's focus is outward: she knows who she is within and, with that, she can stand next to others and not feel separated. She can be the catalyst to unite, just as she has done for friendships at play.

Recently, Barbie has exposed a world out there, with different cities, different pursuits, different timelines, and seeks to identify with them all—as Rani and I may have done in our small, unique, still significant ways.

Like Barbie, Rani and I are not quite done discovering. I still haven't seen India. I have not had a daughter to whom I can bequeath my dolls.

LAST WEEK, WHILE BROWSING FOR GIFTS at the mall, I found myself sifting through the Christmas Angel cards for a little girl who wanted a Barbie. Her name was Jasmine, and she was a year old. At an adjacent toy store, I found a dark-skinned "City Style" Barbie with an A-line burgundy skirt and matching hibiscus patterned shirt. She was sassy, stylish, and smart. And she was on sale. I bought the Barbie and some squishy toys, so Jasmine could first discover the softer elements of life before graduating to the reality of sophistication, of being a girl in America with so much on her mind other than thoughts of what to wear and whom to see, of what and in whom to believe. Perhaps she'll reach for Barbie as muse to fantasize about the future: a rock star, an actress, a politician, a traveler. A wife. A lawyer. A teacher. A writer. She is Rani, she is me.

---

[1] "Barbie," *All Experts Encyclopedia*, n.d., <http://en.allexperts.com/e/b/ba/barbie.htm> (1 May 2007).

[2] "Barbie," *All Experts Encyclopedia*, n.d., <http://en.allexperts.com/e/b/ba/barbie.htm> (1 May 2007).

[3] "'Babyish' Barbie under attack from little girls, study shows." *University of Bath Press Release.* 19 Dec. 2005. <http://www.bath.ac.uk/news/articles/releases/barbie161205.html> (1 May 2007).

[4] Brigitte Greenberg, "The BLO—Barbie Liberation Organization—Strikes." *The Unit Circle*, n.d., <http://www.etext.org/Zines/UnitCircle/uc3/page10.html> (1 May 2007).

[5] "'Jewish' Barbie Dolls Denounced in Saudi Arabia," *Anti-Defamation League: Muslim/Arab World,* 18 Sep. 2003, <http://www.adl.org/main_Arab_World/barbie.htm> (1 May 2007).

[6] Melissa Summers, "Fulla, the Middle East's Bestselling Doll," *ParentDish,* 22 Sep. 2005, <http://www.bloggingbaby.com/2005/09/22/fulla-the-middle-easts-bestselling-doll/> (1 May 2007).

[7] "Looks vs. Credibility," *PBS: Local News*, n.d., <http://www.pbs.org/wnet/insidelocalnews/behind_looks.html> (1 May 2007).

SHE CANNOT REMEMBER SOCRATES S. JASON FRALEY

the day is far from transparent   I am a starlet
a supermodel with windswept bangs matted

to mascara or God has poured packets
of allergen into the atmosphere and is busy

finding a spoon   it depends on the direction
of the wind or if I'm immersed in a script

   I cannot imagine drinking the sky
unless there's a grand operatic movement every time

a mouth opens or when scientists scrawl
supersede over Newton   of course the greatest

surprise may not be the initial ascension   sorry
my anonymity in these black-rimmed glasses inspires

my philosophic side   I slept with a director
who claimed that the lens wasn't a gateway

to the self   rather it's a hollow eye
that immediately forgets my every movement

     he told me to avoid mirrors or the camera's
revelation flash would leave me blind

     and invisible.

BECAUSE THERE IS NO EASY ANSWER S. JASON FRALEY

A group of women

          a cult of sorceresses / a Sapphic society / researchers trying to determine what exactly constitutes a group / a séance to determine who father loved most

gather in a circle

          forearm radii / light always filters in / for expediency, because an octagon is unnecessarily rigid / because they sold their spines to the black market

around a map.

          of the world during the 15th century / of Paris / of every river to discover the absolute lowest point / of themselves in thirty seconds

Thumbtacks and string.

          nodes and pathways / a world without (air)planes / a world after magic / because the rapture would stall if the earth didn't rotate

S. JASON FRALEY

    She reaches into a picnic basket

                                      as if it were a mouth filled with gold bullion / and pulls out an epee / and recites the spell of disassembly to make travel possible / and lifts up her own skirt

    and pulls out an apple

                                      don't think a child reaching for any combination of the following: God, an overripe ovary, a Molotov cocktail, a container of liquid nitrogen

    that she refuses to eat.

                                      it's too beautiful / the queen's dress is the same shade of green / why be responsible for the first blemish / the others are a biased jury / because she covets ghosts

STANDARD AND DISTINCT THINGS GREGORY O'NEILL

Genius only fills the conscious void.
Stars pick up where skyscrapers
leave off. Noah broke a sweat for God,
but he only dripped humanity.
Beyond this architecture of huts
sanguine tongues remain parched. Seeking
to settle the dust of love we pray
for more rain.

JESUS CALLED ELLEN MORRIS PREWITT

Her family had lived in the same spot for over one hundred and fifty years. Her great-grandfather was the first banker in the state; her grandfather's white-columned home received President Taft. Her own father had worn hand-tailored shirts. When he died—she was a grown-up girl by then—she tissued one of her daddy's shirts away, folded and tucked in the closet of her new home.

But she married a man who grew up owning one change of clothes, who was the first in his rural Mississippi family to go to college, whose daddy said, "Un, huh," when Avery told him she was an Episcopalian.

Avery's happiness in love allowed her to rise above these inconsistencies, until the December morning when the sun was still rising and the phone call came from the brother in Scott County.

—It's happened. Granddaddy Frazier died.

So began Avery's reevaluation of love.

The family gathered in Daddy Frazier's convenience store. The store was cold as an ice bucket, its heating system shot. The stale air smelled of re-heated grease while blades of a ceiling fan clicked overhead, flurrying the cramped-in smell. The brother's child, a little Frazier girl, pressed her nose against a display case full of chocolate pudding Sin. The girl's panties shown white from behind. At the end of the glass case slouched a fifty-pound bag of sugar, ready not for the Christmas oven but for the moonshiners' money.

Granny Frazier, the widowed wife of the grandfather, finally arrived, walking ramrod in a tight round hat with tall black feathers. She lifted her chin, looked down on her waiting kin, said,

—Let's hit the blacktop.

Daddy Frazier unplugged the lights to the Tiny Tot Christmas tree, swatted at the string of the unstoppable ceiling fan.

—When I die, guess you'll have to throw my body in the pitch-in and shoot that fan with a shotgun, he said.

Avery's husband laughed. All the Fraziers laughed.

Avery and the Fraziers rode six deep to the funeral home, Avery in the backseat of the old Dodge, shoulder to shoulder with her husband's brother. Avery's husband sat up front, with his bereaved granny. Granny Frazier swerved around a corner. Avery leaned into her brother-in-law, righted herself. Slowly, the Dodge shifted up hill. The Antioch Funeral Home erupted into view. All disembarked.

Inside the door of the funeral home hung a publicity photo of Miss Mississippi. The neckline on her gown angled so low you could see the shadow of a nipple. Every male Frazier paused to absorb the moment.

In the visitation room, a bald-headed Frazier leaned over the casket, said,

—Well, that's the end of it, rite 'cher. By the time he died, even the drunks at Linnie's was tired of singing with him.

Rows of Fraziers filled the folding chairs—no one saying a word, each just claiming a seat. A dumpy old lady Frazier waddled from flower spray to flower spray, reading the cards. When she arrived at Daddy Frazier's heart-shaped spray with the plastic phone in the center, she wagged her head in sorrow. She patted the tacky little phone, ran her hand down the cord to the receiver dangling off its hook. Underneath the receiver, a banner glittered loud: JESUS CALLED HIM HOME.

Avery stationed herself in the hallway, away from the visitation room, away from the folding chairs full of Fraziers. There, she listened to a group of junior undertakers talk about funeral-related merchandise. One of undertakers, a Frazier cousin, caught her eye, gave her the once-over.

—You look ol' Ray up when you're done here, he said.

He fingered the gold chain that snaked the ridge of his collarbone.

Avery slipped on her dark glasses, turned her head.

Narrow windows hung high in the funeral home walls. Breaking rain popped against the slitted glass.

The night Avery was to marry, her mother had accosted her in the outer vestibule of the church. Gripping Avery by the arm, she reminded her daughter of the heritage she'd received through her deceased father: the white-columned house, the hand-tailored life. "Throwing it away on . . . these people," her mother had hissed.

But Avery refused to listen to anything her mother had to say about her husband. She cared only that on walks through the fields, Granny Frazier had made her young grandson carry a peach limb in case he thought about being bad. The little tow-headed boy who would become

Avery's husband—head down, dragging his switch through the dirt—him Avery would love forever, and ignore the rest.

A woman holding a baby Frazier sidled down the hallway, passing an aunt. The aunt wobbled for the baby, pantomiming Granddaddy Frazier's pickled death.

—He wobbled a little, then just fell over.

When the woman and the baby passed Avery, the baby gurgled, reached with its dirty fingers, tried to swat Avery's dark glasses. The woman smiled, tentative, like maybe Avery wasn't a Frazier. Avery never smiled back, making her think she was right.

A wail gushed from the visitation room: the widow's rising, obligatory grief.

—Oh, Poppa. Oh, Poppa.

Avery, beaten, stepped into the room to call an end to the visit. Over by the casket, her husband stood attentive beside his grandmother. His patting hand lightly comforted the old woman's trembling back. He whispered something in his granny's ear. When he straightened, he brushed his bangs from his eyes, caught his wife looking. He smiled, full of love.

Avery sank, slowly, into a folding chair.

That evening—after the burying and the grave site and the gathering in the home—Avery sat in the passenger seat of the car, far away from her husband as he drove them back to the city. In her ears rang the sputtering of the graveside preacher, cursing the unrepentant drunkard:

—If your hand or your foot causes you to sin, cut it off and throw it away. Better to enter the kingdom of heaven without your right arm than to fall whole into the pits of hell.

Outside the car window, the red clay hills undulated.

Back at home, Avery removed the painting of the white-columned house from her living room wall, turned it face-down on the closet floor. Her father's hand-tailored shirt—the one she'd saved in tissue until now—she slipped around her shoulders.

She stroked the cotton, smooth as sateen. Then, with the preacher's ringing words in her ears, she ripped off the right arm, watched as the threads frayed across the seam.

The ripped sleeve she lay on her husband's side of the bed, waiting for him to walk in, flick on the light, see the empty sleeve upon its offering place.

The remainder of the shirt she re-folded in the tissue, put in the next morning's mail. When her mother opened the package Christmas day, she held up the one-armed shirt, called her daughter on the phone for an explanation of such a gift.

But Avery and her husband were busy celebrating the awakening of the morning. Avery lifted the receiver, dropped it beside the bed. There, it dangled off its hook.

BOYS OF IONA PREP ANN CEFOLA

Slick cuts and cumbersome jackets,
they dawdle in early and odd-numbered adolescence,
waiting for the Christian Brothers' van to spirit them away.
Every day, they fix on the dim theater of my car
where my husband and I unroll like film:
They freeze for the parting press of our lips.

In Su Young's Coffeeshop, one of them sits
in the dark as the retirees eat
their scrambled eggs and smoke.
Mid-kiss I catch his eye unblinking
and I am no longer being but body,
marriage no longer a distant vow

but wet contact. I want to wink or wave at him
like Venus toying with tin soldiers,
or bless him with a bare breast.
Anointing him with
the chrism of desire,
I sing, *Holy, holy, holy,*
Blessed is he.

ST. AGNES, PINKSLIPPED ANN CEFOLA

Hospital changes name to Westchester Medical Center, White Plains Pavillion.
    —May 2003

Walking past forsythia, magnolia, dogwood, over the soft bed of cherry blossoms shed,
she wonders if this is what she most wanted to avoid:
    the consolation of angels.

Did you see her hitching along North Street? Melted halo liquid light around her neck,
once golden raiment a yellow raincoat, hovering toes now firmly bound in sneakers.
    Recalling newborns

she coaxed into sterile birthroom light; children, bald, bleeding, incubated,
who healed at her radiant grin, the aged whose trembling hands she'd grasp,
    telling them: *Heaven! Imagine!*

And they: *Okay, my last breath.* Then *No, please another look.*
Finally, their resigned: *Let's go.*
    Thinking about that envelope

left by the CEO. Some younger nurses wept and Colombian gardeners crossed themselves,
muttering, *¡Dios mio!* before delicately removing her statues throughout the grounds.
    Interceding on her own behalf,

she asks for work as a home health aide, local apparition or might she replace
a negligent guardian angel? Anything not to lose the perfume of seasons,
    like the lilac she brushes

her wet face against, the very air she breathes a vibrant green vapor,
and tulips her eyes widen to take in
    like the holiest red and gold robes.

ST. AGNES, PINKSLIPPED

Now she understands the dilemma of the dying: how they don't want to turn
their backs on the sun-edged bloom, how one human spring
    can ruin paradise.

DILL JILL KANDEL

Licking his finger he smiles down at his donut. He swipes the frosting and brings spit-glued sprinkles up to his mouth. As his tongue slides out through front teeth that arch forward in an elliptical overbite, he licks his finger again. It is hard not to stare. He reminds me of Dill in *To Kill a Mockingbird*, tiny mouth and scrawny arms. We are the only two sitting down for breakfast at the long table. Food sticks to his braces. Behind the many-hued sprinkles, his teeth are yellow.

"I'm a sugar freak," he says, pouring sugar onto his dazzling lucky loops cereal. It's hard to talk when my eyes are mesmerized by his teeth, now sugarcoated with a strawberry loop attached like a miniature hula-hoop.

"I live with Grandmamother—she adopted me—I came from California—my mother's in Arizona—Grandmamother brought me to camp—I'm a sugar freak—I've never been to camp before—what are we going to do for a whole week?" His quick staccato speech halts while he pours more sugar, this time into his hot chocolate.

He stares at me and stirs. I want to gag.

I tap the sugar jar with my index finger. "It's not good for you," I say. "You've had enough."

"I'm a sugar freak."

"I know," I reply. "Eat some eggs."

The dining room is filling up with campers. Chairs scrape across the cement floor. Kids mumble. Counselors grab coffee. I snatch the sugar jar and shove it away.

"Too bad there aren't any marshmallows—for the hot chocolate—that would make it better—I like the colored mini ones."

"Do you like to play soccer?" I ask wondering why he's come to camp.

"I don't know—I never played before—yesterday was my first try—this chocolate is too hot—I can't drink it—adding sugar would cool it off."

"Try some milk instead," I say.

I give him his morning pills: Prozac for depression, Benadryl for allergies, Claritin for hay fever, and Ritalin; he's hyperactive. Dill swallows them willingly then pushes and prods his food. Only sugar and pills are allowed to pass though his pursed lips where drawbridge braces guard his tiny mouth. The mushy red cereal has turned his yellow teeth into an orange grin, like he's taken the peel off an orange wedge and made a fake smile, flashing it at others, Ha! Look at my orange teeth. Plastic red lips. Vampire fangs. Boys laugh and high-five. You scared the girls! But Dill does not achieve such a response. He isn't artificial.

Campers sprint by with bananas, orange juice, and bagels. Shouts echo across the room. A camper comes over, "Hey nurse, you gotta Band-Aid? I got this blister thing here."

"Let's have a look," I say to him. This is what I do the most. I look at feet. I pull off grimy socks and check heel blisters, between-the-toes blisters, I-just-bought-new-cleats blisters. I disinfect feet that are bruised, calloused, weeping, and bloody. I enjoy looking at feet. I hold them exposed in my hand as I examine the tender underbellies of sweaty arches, trim off deadened skin, and meddle out offending particles of sand and pebble. I find the soft pink purity underneath the injury. Skin is resilient. If cleaned well, it will repair itself.

"Let's go over to the infirmary," I say.

Dill sits alone.

I have a bevy of Band-Aids available: spray on, waterproof, wet-flex with extra foam cushioning, non-sticking, and sheer. They are anywhere from ⅞th inch mini squares to 4 inch pads. They occupy a full shelf at the infirmary and I am fastidious to choose just the right one and fix the offending sore correctly.

This particular blister is in a difficult location. "I'll put some liquid Band-Aid on it," I say, as I analyze, clean, and cut. I paint thick clear liquid onto clean skin.

"Looks great," I tell the camper. "Make a goal for me."

"Sure thing, Nurse," he replies, already out the door.

I should be satisfied, but I can't get Dill out of my thoughts as I pass out sun screen and rub greasy balm into sore muscles. He irritates my mind. I dig around and can't get hold of this sugar-baby child with his problems that last the whole day, and the next and the next. He distresses me simply because I am so confident. I want to clean him out and fix him up.

But nothing on my shelves will change his reality.

When he leaves camp he will go back to an elderly, fill-in mother. He will continue his life of sugar highs and medicated comforts. These are the Band-Aids that patch over his festering sores.

I imagine him drinking sodas, slurping gummy worms, and swallowing sugar-coated pills. I see him on the side lines of life, sitting on a bench beside a sixty year old woman. In the stands are the other mothers—in their twenties—who are cheering for their sons out on the soccer field. I see him at the pharmacy, standing beside an aging woman, carrying a grocery sack full of medications. I see him at the orthodontist. The doctor is taking off Dill's braces. Underneath the silver wires his teeth are pocked with holes.

I see Dill everyday. I cannot let him go. Late at night, when I am tired, I imagine God holding Dill by the scruff of his neck. He holds him high above the tiny world and gently lowers him. As He does so God knows what He is doing. Dill the odd, the magnificent, the different is set down by a loving Hand. God sees a graying grandmother and places Dill into her arms, ready or not. I fall asleep with her image in my mind. She can't help but smile. She tucks a blue fleece blanket under his tiny chin.

SECOND WHITSUN MAUREEN TOLMAN FLANNERY

When the day of Pentecost came . . . Tongues
as of fire appeared, which parted and came
to rest on each of them. They began to express
themselves in foreign tongues.
    —Acts 2:1–4

It might be some late May morning not unlike this one,
fat yellow sun in its high place, blue breezes
drifting off to sleep beside still green leaves,
and suddenly out of the sky will come
noises like a driving wind. A bright white bird,
fuel of what words can do ablaze on its feathers,
will burn down upon us like meteor showers
and we will understand each other in amazement,
being from scattered lands and being combatively close,
being Palestinians and settlers of the West Bank,
Ulster Protestant and Nationalist, Indian and Pakistani.
There will be among us autonomy-over-one's-bodyists
and soul-from-the-moment-of-conceptionists,
ranchers and vegetarians,
hunters and lobbyists for animal rights,
recent graduates of School of the Americas,
malleable minded soldiers,
and women left in the villages from which
los desaparados have disappeared,
men laid off and eager executives
paid to find ways to cut costs.
We, descended upon by the gift of hearing,
will be from Israel, Lebanon, Egypt,
and regions of Libya around Cyrene.

SECOND WHITSUN

There will be among us visitors from Nicaragua
and El Salvador, *Zapotistas* and *Federales*
and desperate young men recruited into death squads,
homeless women and software consultants,
Republican Senators and needle sharers,
the dying, their doctors, and creators of managed care.
We will be Hutu and Tutsi,
Croat, Serb, Muslim, Albanian,
farmers on homesteaded land and
scientists in labs of genetic research,
women in *hijab*, women in beguiling veils of silk chiffon,
women in Victoria's Secret under jeans,
killers and the loved ones of their victims,
paper pushers and CEOs, supremacists,
extremists, and believers in redeemers,
each of us understanding the tongues of others,
for the Word will pour Itself into us,
and we will have ears to hear it.

SAINTS OF COLORADO CHRISTOPHER ESSEX

CARL WAS BAPTIZING AGAIN. My friend had coaxed some dandelion-haired six-year-old out into the water and he had one hand on the back of the head of the leaned-over kid. Carl had a worn leather-bound copy of the Bible in the other hand and was saying something over the boy. It was not the first time I'd seen the ceremony, not the first time I'd seen my friend standing in a flowing white gown he'd made from an old bedsheet which drifted as the waves of river water tugged it to and fro. I knelt down on the edge of the river bed, on the grass. I didn't want to interrupt him, knowing how seriously he took the ceremony, and his religion in general. Just as I was starting to get some of the words as they came to me across the water, they were drowned out by the loud, angry voice of a man who stepped out from the trees behind me.

"Kelly!" the man shouted. "You get over here! You get away from him!" He stomped out into the water in his work boots as his young son straightened up and looked at his father with wide eyes. The man splashed out to where the boys were and grabbed his son's hand.

"He's been baptized already just fine, Carl Matthews," the man told my friend. "He doesn't need you doing it again." He pulled his son along behind him as he made his way back to the shore. The man glared at me as he passed.

Carl stood in the water watching them leave, passing through the stand of trees and then out onto the street, where they disappeared from view. His face was a mixture of dismay and disappointment. Then he looked at me, and a flicker of hope crossed his features.

"Oh, no," I said, standing up, shaking my head, backing up a few steps. "Don't even ask. I'm not giving up my agnosticism for anything."

Carl frowned but nodded, and then, seeing that no other possible baptismal candidates were in view, started trudging towards shore. When he came onto the grassy bank, I saw that he was barefoot. The wet, nearly transparent cloth clung to his legs where it had been in the water. He handed me the Bible and reached down and pulled up the white gown, past his hips, over his shoulders and off. I could see the stitching, which, given its roughness, was probably his own work. I had never seen the gown before. When he had first begun his baptisms, he had worn his mother's wedding gown, believe it or not, but when she found out, that practice of course quickly ended. "I don't understand it," he had said to me. "It's not like she's ever going to wear it again."

Now, wearing his bright yellow T-shirt, bluejean shorts and the sneakers he pressed his bare feet into, the thin boy with his short brown hair and glasses gave a much more convincing imitation of a normal fourteen-year-old kid. I handed him back the Bible and he took it in the hand that wasn't carrying the folded-up gown. We walked together through the trees and out onto the street.

"Once again, why are you doing this?" I asked him. "It's not just an excuse to wear white dresses, right?"

Carl smiled slightly and shook his head, in a dignified manner, and addressed me like a professor explaining something to one of his duller students. "It's not that I want to do this, Jeremy. Have you ever felt like you couldn't not do something? Like some power stronger than your own was guiding you, whispering in your ear exactly what you needed to do next and how to do it, like some unseen hand was guiding yours?"

I shook my head. "Not since that time they gave me the wrong prescription instead of my Ritalin."

Just then there was giggling, and I saw Carl frown. Two girls were walking down this street towards us, one side of the street angling down towards the water and the other side being small houses, with their driveways and mailboxes, cars and bikes. Both girls were wearing shorts and T-shirts, just like us, but to an entirely different effect.

"Well, look who's here, down by the river, my stupid little brother and his cute friend." Valerie walked up to us and put her arm around my shoulders, provocatively. "Look at Jeremy, Barbara" she told her friend. "He's getting a blood sausage. I think he likes us."

Barbara just scowled at us both, as if they'd just come upon a particularly grisly roadkill.

Valerie's tall, heavy body leaned into me, almost making my knees collapse. "He wasn't bothering more kids down by the river, was he? You know he was almost in the paper last week about that. Dad had to call the reporter and give him a discount on an engine rebuild to kill the story."

I had heard about that. Carl's dad was an upstanding member of the community, a small business owner and generally a very sensible man. He didn't even begin to understand his son. But who did?

I opened my mouth to respond but Carl spoke up instead. "Go away, Valerie and Barbara," he said. "Leave us alone."

Valerie ignored her brother. "Maybe we should go over to your place, Jeremy. We saw your father leaving town. In his old pickup truck."

"He's only had it for four years," I protested. "It's not an old pickup truck."

"Fine," she said, her breath in my ear. "His brand new four year old pickup truck. Where is he going all the time? I thought he worked here in town but he's always leaving. I see his truck heading out of town all the time."

"He fishes," I said.

"You don't fish at three o'clock in the afternoon," she said. "I think he's having an affair, Barbara. His father's a handsome man, all right. But that's not the interesting thing I know about you. In fact, it's not even the most interesting." She took her arm away and stood in front of me, stopping my forward progress. Her breasts were right at my face level and I had to quickly stop to avoid crashing into them.

"What?" I said, annoyance in my voice and eyes. I hated guessing games.

"He has no clue," she told her friend. Barbara, who was even taller than Valerie but with less padding upstairs, just nodded, obviously very bored with this scene. "He has totally no clue."

"What?" I repeated.

"You should close your bedroom window at night," she said, with a smile.

"So, you've been peeking in my window, so what?" I said angrily. I pushed past her.

"Not me," Valerie said, with an offended attitude. "If I wanted to see your little weenie, I'd just ask. No, it's not me. Think about your new neighbors. I hear things have been getting darker in your neighborhood. And not just at night."

I frowned, confused. What was she talking about?

"Just think about it," she said, as she and Barbara resumed walking in the other direction. "Think about it and close your drapes tonight. Or keep them open, see what I care." I walked quickly away from them, and without looking back, heard Carl catching up behind me.

"She can see right into your room at night," Valerie shouted, loud enough for everyone in the neighborhood to hear. "She likes you, Joelle does."

I LIKED BEING IN THE PICKUP TRUCK with my father. I liked the smell of his cigarettes and the mess of fast food wrappers at my feet that mushed down when you stepped on them. I liked the way the pickup had a stick transmission while Mom's car had an automatic. Dad would even let me drive it sometimes, which I really enjoyed. But mostly, I liked being in Dad's pickup because he would talk, which he didn't do much around the house.

It was the day after my disturbing discussion with Valerie, and I was doing my best of forget it ever happened. I was sorting through a handful of baseball cards, and the sun was beaming through the scarred windshield as my father muscled the wheel around the ever-curving, ever-rising road. The truck rumbled and bounced me around and shifted me from side to side as I tightly held onto the cards. We were up above treeline now and the landscape looked something like Mars, barren and dry and brown and cold, as opposed to the dark green lushness of the landscape we had just passed through.

I had another two packs of cards in my jacket pocket, unopened. I badly wanted to see what cards were in them, but I didn't dare pull them out. I had stolen the cards from the gas station at the edge of town, right under my dad's nose as he paid for the gas. When I had pulled out the first pack and opened it, he had commented that he hadn't noticed me buying them. I told him I had, while he was in the restroom. I wasn't sure if he suspected my secret hobby or not, but I couldn't risk pulling the other two packs out; he knew I didn't have enough money for three packs of cards.

My stealing habit was an ever-present source of guilt and shame for me, but I was hopelessly addicted. I didn't really care what I stole most of the time, and sometimes I would end up just giving or throwing away my ill-gotten goods. It wasn't the having, but the taking that was exciting, and so fulfilling. The adrenaline rush when you slipped whatever it was into the pocket of your loose pants, or up the sleeve of your jacket, or even better, that incredible moment when you were outside the store in the sun of the parking lot and it was yours, whatever it was that you hadn't paid for. I knew it was inevitable that I would get caught one day, if I didn't give up this habit, but I was helpless in the face of it.

Carl knew about my shameful hobby. I had confessed to him a few weeks back. He shook his head sadly, but his eyes weren't condemning. "It feels better to tell someone, doesn't it?" he said.

I nodded my head. It did feel better. But it didn't feel that much better. Not as good as sinning again would, I knew that.

"I have some money," he said. "Next time you feel like stealing, tell me and I'll buy it for you."

It was nice of him to say. I knew he didn't have any more money than I did, as our allowances were about the same every week. It wasn't that I needed the things I stole, anyway.

"This is such beautiful country up here," my father said, as the truck rumbled along the road. The sun had disappeared within a shapeless mass of thick white clouds that seemed to hang only a few feet above us. We had long ago ceased to see any human dwellings and little plant or animal life was visible, either, but my father's smile was an honest one. He pulled over to the dusty side of the road, though he could have just stopped where we were, as there wasn't another vehicle in view. "Get out and take a look around," he said, shutting off the engine.

I put my cards away in my pocket and opened the door. Immediately, I clutched my jacket around me as a bitter wind blew into the cab of the truck. I stepped quickly outside, slamming the door behind me. I walked over to the driver's side of the vehicle, where my father was leaning against the truck, a freshly lit cigarette in hand, staring out at the mountainous vista in front of us, the brown tops of the higher mountains, which would have had snow on them except that our winter was exceptionally dry that year, and the dark green valley below. I could see a few specks that were cabins or houses down in the green.

"One of these days I'm not going back down there," my father said.

"What?" I responded. My voice was dry and harsh. I had to keep brushing my hair out of my eyes as the cold wind whipped it around. I looked at my father's features. He was not an emotional man, and you could see that by looking at him. He looked stern and unfriendly, I had heard others say, but it wasn't that he was mean or unkind—he just didn't seem to have the need for other people the way most people did. I loved my father, but I needed to love him more than he needed to be loved.

We stood there by the truck for a long time, and finally I said, "Can we go home now?"

My father turned and looked at me, his eyebrows high, looking surprised to see me there next to him. He nodded, stubbed out his cigarette on the road and got back into the truck. I hurried around to my side and got in. My father turned the key in the ignition and for a scary moment nothing happened. Just silence. But then he tried again and the engine started. I reached for the heater controls and turned it up high. He cranked the steering wheel around and we headed back to town.

That night, after my bath, I walked into my room with just a towel on, and I happened to glance towards the window. The window was above my desk, which was piled with mostly stolen junk. The dusty drapes hung on either side, and in the entire time we had lived in the house, I don't think I had ever bothered to close them. The view from them was unexceptional, and I seldom looked out the window; you saw a couple of trees, the old chainlink fence, and the side of the next house over. I stepped over to the window now and peered outside. Of course, what I mostly saw was myself, since the room was brightly lit, my face and my bare torso, but I also noticed, for the first time, the two windows on the house beside ours. Neither of them were lit, but there was a car in the driveway, and I knew there could be people behind those windows, looking out. I thought about it for a moment, and then I backed away from the window, and like every night in the past, started getting into my pajamas. But I have to admit, I did feel a little bit different about it. It added a little edge of excitement to a boring task, a boring life.

During our walk to school the next morning, Carl reached into his pocket and pulled out something. "Hey," he said. "Do you know what this is?"

I figured he was showing me a nasty piece of candy covered in lint that he couldn't identify. He wore the same blue jeans every day, with its knees faded nearly to pure white. Whatever it was could have been there for years. I looked down at his hand, and saw a small, thin, gray bone resting in the palm, about an inch long.

"You had chicken last night," I said.

"Look again," he said. "It's not a chicken bone."

He stopped and I bent down to look at it closer.

"It's a relic," Carl said. "Haven't you seen a relic before? Of course you haven't, not living in this town, not living the life you lead."

"Hey!" I protested. "I've lived a life as good as most people. Better than most." But of course the shame of my shoplifting hobby came to the surface for a moment. I ignored it.

Carl gave me a smile that showed he wasn't buying it. "It's the fingerbone of a saint," he said. And then he closed his fingers around it again and started walking once more.

"Yeah, right," I said, walking along with him. It was a beautiful morning, and I looked up at the bright blue sky. I was about to ask him if he had done the math homework, when he spoke again.

"Saint Jeffrey of Ward," Carl said solemnly.

"You're full of it," I replied. Ward is a town in the mountains not too far from here. It has a couple of bars and a little general store and about eight houses, maybe nine. "Ward's full of old hippies," I said. "Did someone in Ward tell you that was the fingerbone of a saint? I heard they spend all their time in Ward doing mushrooms. You shouldn't talk to people from Ward."

Carl laughed lightly and pocketed the bone again. "It's a sacred artifact," he said, as if I were a small, stupid child. "You can recognize the men who know God by the relics that they possess." He sounded like he was quoting something, but of course I didn't know what.

"You're not a man," I pointed out. "And you've got a chicken bone in your pocket."

We were nearing the little strip mall that we always passed on the way to school. It had a pizza place, a video store, a travel agency, a ski/backpacking equipment store, and a grocery store, the last being the setting of most of my illicit escapades. I nodded towards it and said, "You want to go in?"

"What, you want to steal something?" Carl said. I winced. He was getting back at me for not believing in his relic. I felt bad for dismissing it so harshly. I felt even worse, though, because he was right; I did want to steal something. It was gnawing at me, somewhere deep inside. I hadn't taken anything since the baseball cards the day before. I looked over at the door of the store longingly, at all the goods inside its windows. But Carl just kept walking towards school and reluctantly I followed him. But I knew I would be back there, in that store, before the day was over.

WE HAD GYM CLASS THAT DAY. I never minded gym class, like some kids did, because I had a big dick and so the other guys didn't pick on me or tease me. It was silly how something like that made a difference but it did. But running and jumping and catching balls, the things we did in gym, never interested me that much. I would forget about the goal of the game—kicking the ball in a certain direction, for instance—and just be standing out in the middle of the field, thinking my own thoughts—like what I might steal that afternoon—and the ball would come skittering towards me, with my classmates storming along behind it, and I would just let it pass or give it a kick in what would always turn out to be the wrong direction.

As it turned out, we were playing soccer again today. Most of the kids in my grade were on soccer teams and they always complained when we didn't play the game. Mr. Howard, our old gym coach, had some spine and we only played the game when it came up in our regular rotation, but Mr. Williams was a wimp and let the students have their way most of the time. He was a new teacher and his students basically owned him.

As we walked out to the field, Carl came up behind me. His arms and legs looked very pale as he walked along in his T-shirt and shorts. His father had bought him some expensive soccer shoes, in the hopes that he would take up this hobby instead, and so Carl was walking along in these shoes that were the most expensive thing he owned

"He saved the lives of seven children, you know," Carl said. "From a horrible, horrible fire. What have you done with your life?"

"It isn't over," I told him. Frankly, I was getting a little annoyed with this weirdo priest-boy. I walked faster and caught up with some other classmates, and started talking with them.

Somewhere around the middle of the game, I heard someone calling my name.

"Daniel," the voice said. "Your name is Daniel, right?"

I looked behind me and saw a girl with skin the color of coffee with cream in it. Her hair was in black braids like licorice whips and she had dark, deep eyes. She was wearing the same sort of thing as the rest of us, but I noticed that she had bright pink socks on. "Yeah," I said. "That's me."

"My name's Joelle," she said.

"Yeah, I know," I said. "Hi." I made an effort to be visibly watching the game, watching as a cluster of my classmates chased the ball from here to there, never getting very close to a goal.

"It's not true," she said. "What they say. Those girls made it up."

"What?" I said, my voice a little shaky. "Made what up?"

"You know, about me looking through your window at you. I would never do something like that. I could, but I wouldn't. That's just plain rude."

"Okay, thanks for telling me," I said. The ball was moving in our general direction and I felt like everyone was watching me. I tensed up and got ready to run after the ball.

"Those girls just don't like me. I never done anything to them, either," she said. "You know why they don't like me."

I nodded. I did know. "Don't let it bother you," I said. "They don't like anyone."

"That's not true," Joelle said. "There's plenty of people they like. But not people like me."

"Uh-huh," I said. There was no arguing with that.

"Well," Joelle said, and she took a step away from me. "I just wanted to tell you that. I promise I won't look in the direction of your window at night."

"Okay," I said. "That's fine." I was surprised at the sound of my voice, the tone of it, and she looked a little surprised, too. Was that the sound of disappointment in my voice? The ball came in my direction and I ran for it.

I walked home from school with Carl, like usual. "Can you come over to my house?" he asked, as we were getting our jackets and bookbags from our lockers. "I need your help with something."

"Okay," I said.

"Mom? Dad? Valerie?" Carl shouted as we entered the house, and we paused a moment, but there was no response other than a dim echo. He smiled to himself and led me to his bedroom. Once inside the room, he reached under his bed and pulled out a long, shallow cardboard box. He put it on the bed and opened it. Inside I saw his Bible, the white gown he had made, two half-used candles in tarnished silver candlestick holders, and a plastic wineglass. He lifted the gown up out of the box and started to put it on. I turned away from this intimate activity and looked out his window.

"Okay," he said after a moment. "I'll be right back." He walked out of the room in his white gown and quickly returned, with a jar of Welch's Grape Juice in one hand and a box of Nilla wafers in the other.

"Don't you have apple?" I said. "I don't really like grape juice."

He frowned. "I don't think apple juice would work. Sorry."

"Some chips would be nice, too," I said, looking unhappily at the Nilla wafers box.

"Look," Carl said sternly. "The body of Christ can't be a sour-cream-and-chive potato chip, okay? There are certain rules to this ceremony."

"What ceremony?" I said.

"Communion, of course," he said. "I've never done this before, I need to practice."

"What?" I said, disbelief in my voice. "What are you going to be doing next? Circumcision?"

"Circumcision is a Jewish ritual, Daniel," my friend said. He picked up his Bible and was paging through it. "Anyway, you've already been through it."

"Can't you do this with your family?" I said.

"Oh, they're lifelong Protestants," he said. "They don't understand."

"You're an unusual kid, Carl," I said, opening the box of wafers. I took out one of the thin, vanilla-flavored cookies and bit into it. I quickly ate several cookies; I usually had some sort of snack about this time every day. I poured some grape juice into the plastic wine glass.

"Hey, save that for the ceremony," Carl said. He put down the Bible and set up the candles on either side of his desk. He quickly lit them from a pack of matches that he pulled out of his pockets. He walked up to me and grabbed both shoulders. "Okay, stand right here," he said, positioning me a few feet from the desk, facing it. "Can you kneel down?"

I nodded and knelt down on one knee. Carl stood in front of me and picked up his Bible and started reading from it. The drapes behind him were drawn but the sun still shown through the fabric, giving the room a yellowish tint, and the candles brightly flickered. Carl's face looked soft and young in this light, and his voice was strangely calming. Even in this awkward position, I started to drift off.

After awhile, Carl put down the Bible and picked up the glass of grape juice and a Nilla wafer and stepped closer to me. I looked up at him but his eyes were strangely distant. "Are you ready to receive the body and the blood of our Lord?"

Without even the thought of refusing, I nodded my head and he stepped closer to me. I opened my mouth.

"What the hell is going on here?" a loud voice said. It was Carl's father, standing in the doorway of the bedroom.

"Shit," Carl said, his voice and face completely normal now. I quickly stood up, my face red from the effort and the embarrassment. Everyone stood there silently for a moment, while the candles flickered, reflecting off of Carl's father's bald head. His glaring eyes looked around the room.

"I can't believe you, Carl," his father said finally. "Where do you get this from? I was never like this as a kid."

"It comes from the Lord, Dad," Carl said, glancing upwards for a moment.

The man just stared at him, as he stood there in his long white gown, until he finally shook his head and walked out of the room.

After his father was gone, Carl pulled off the gown and sat down heavily on the bed with a scowl on his face. He took a sip of the grape juice and bit the wafer in half.

"Is this a fun game to play?" I asked quietly.

"It's not a game, Daniel," he said.

I nodded and, after a moment, got up and left the room.

I WAS WALKING DOWN ONE OF THE LONG AISLES of the store trying to decide what to take when I saw her. Joelle was there with her family. I stayed behind them a safe distance, just staring at her. I couldn't get used to looking at her; her bright smile, dark eyes and pink socks just seemed to lead me through the store. She was talking with her big sister and didn't notice my stalking of her as they shopped. Finally, as they got in line, I could take no more and I walked outside. Only when I was out in the sunshine again did I stick my hands in my jacket pockets and remember I hadn't bothered to take anything.

She came out through the automatic door and saw me as I stood by the newspaper machine. "Hi, Daniel," she said.

I had the urge to run but I stood my ground. "Hi, Joelle," I said.

"I'll be right there, Kara," she said to her sister and the older girl walked away, though she stared at me as she left. "I kept my promise," she said as soon as we were alone.

"What do you want from the store?" I asked. "I'll get you something."

"I'm okay," she said. "We just bought a lot of stuff." She gestured towards her family, who were unloading a cart full of groceries into the back of a minivan.

"Anything you want," I said. "Anything in the store."

She looked at the store window for a moment. "Well, you could get me a candy bar, I guess," she said. "My parents wouldn't let me get one."

"It's yours." I stepped towards the door. "Will you be here when I get back?"

"You'll have to hurry," she said, glancing back towards the minivan.

I was back in less than a minute, and I pulled a Hershey's bar out from inside my jacket sleeve.

"Thanks," Joelle said. Just then her sister shouted her name, leaning out of her window from inside the vehicle, and we quickly said goodbye.

"I saw that, Daniel," a familiar voice behind me said. I froze, and for a moment I thought it was all over. But there, stepping through the automatic door, was Valerie. Right behind her was her friend. Barbara, once again, wasn't happy to see me. It was obvious from her expression. They were both wearing shirts that showed off their flat stomachs, and it was hard for me not to stare at Valerie's bellybutton.

"How come you're not stealing candy bars for me, huh?" Valerie asked, pretending to be jealous.

I just shrugged.

"I guess peeking in people's windows pays off," Valerie said. Barbara whispered something into Valerie's ear and they both giggled together. As they stood there in front of me, their hands at their sides, their fingers touched and then linked together. For some reason, seeing the girls holding hands fascinated me.

"Aren't you hanging out with Carl this afternoon?" Valerie asked.

"I was over at your place earlier," I said.

"You left, huh?" she said. "Isn't my brother getting weirder every day? You're pretty normal, Daniel. Why do you hang out with him? You look all right, you don't have warts or anything, and you're intelligent."

"Carl's intelligent," I said.

She shook her head. "Too intelligent for his own good. Really, Daniel. Find some regular guys to be friends with. For your own sake. A year from now, the ways things are going, no one will talk to Carl. They'll cross the street when they see him coming."

"They do that now," the normally silent Barbara said. "Let's go," she said, pulling Valerie by the hand.

"Think about what I said, Daniel," Valerie said, as she started walking away. "For your own sake. I don't want to see you end up like him. You still have a chance to be normal."

AS I WAS WALKING SLOWLY HOME, with Valerie's words still in my ears, I stopped at a busy intersection and waited for the traffic to pass so that I could cross. Out of the corner of my eye, I saw a familiar red pickup heading out of town and I flagged it down. My father nodded to me. I got in, he put the truck into gear, and we headed towards the sky.

LETTER TO THE CHURCHES CHRISTOPHER MULROONEY

let us see to the churches
and doors and absconding ruffians
the vague interests
and archetypes
we have considered
as at all events
we have considered
also
you

here is the tintype
we have all stood still for
in grand reflection

ESTHER: A REMEMBRANCE RICHARD WILE

Newly licensed as a Lay Reader and Chalice Bearer, I sit at the front of the church, four steps above the rest of the congregation, across from Father Appleyard, both of us surrounded by mahogany woodwork, golden candlesticks, and red upholstery. I feel as if I'm on stage for my first real performance: Palm Sunday and the reading of "The Passion of our Lord Jesus Christ According to Saint Mark." Self-consciously, I finger my new cross. I note Father Appleyard's ramrod posture and I throw my shoulders back. Jonathan runs his services with military precision and I'm afraid of screwing up. I worry about when to go up to the altar. I worry about spilling wine on the red, green, and white altar cloth, or worse, of spilling on someone like Marge Follansbee of the Altar Guild.

Suddenly, the congregation cries, "Crucify him!"

I flinch, realize they aren't passing judgement on me, and hurry to find my place in the reading. I've been going to this church for five years now and I still don't understand why we read the story of Jesus' betrayal and crucifixion on Palm Sunday, right after we've sung "All Glory, Laud, and Honor" and waved palm branches into the air. I don't like having to take the role of one of the mocking crowd. I've already been Peter and denied my Lord three times; now I have to join the aging congregation screaming for Jesus' execution. Still, when it's time to read the words again, my voice rings through the church with the others: "Crucify him!"

I hear shrill voices chanting in my head: "Fart-smeller Morin!" Shards of an image: two wide eyes darting around the classroom . . . a tangled head of dark hair. I try to summon faces, but what comes first is my desk in the back row—second row from the window, third row from the blackboard—bolted to the floor, a hole in it for an inkwell, gouged with initials, hearts, crosses, and maybe even a skull and cross-bones.

Fourth—no, third grade: our teacher, Mrs. Croudis, showing us how to fold a piece of math-paper into a boat. First we make something that looks like a hat, and then a four-sided cone. Next we're supposed to fold the sides of the cone into a boat, but before we get that far, I hear Mary Barker giggle. Craig Pride has put the cone over his nose and mouth. I don't understand. He takes the paper away from his face and points at Esther Morin sitting against the wall. He grabs his neck and sticks out his tongue and gags. Then he pulls the paper cone over his nose and mouth and breathes deeply. Oh, I get it—a gas mask! I gag the way Craig does, put my cone over my nose, and sigh contentedly. He smiles and nods. Soon we have a bunch of guys pointing, gagging, and breathing into gas masks. Giggling erupts into laughter. When Esther sees what's going on, her eyes widen like some frightened animal's. She puts her head down on the desk.

God, it's been forty years since I've thought about Esther Morin. What else do I remember? She was taller than the rest of us, thin, round-shouldered, with a long face. I want to say she had bad teeth. I picture a faded dress, probably too short to cover her scabby knees, dirty socks puddled around her ankles, and scuffed shoes with at least one broken strap. I know she was older than the rest of us, possibly even twelve or thirteen. I'm sure she had serious learning disabilities.

She probably smelled of smoke and fish, because I think she grew up in "Grantville," a cluster of tarpaper shacks and rotting houses by the shore belonging to poor fishermen and clammers, most of whom were or had been Grants. Her mother, then, must have been a Grant before she married Harold Morin, a carpenter my father considered "number than a pounded thumb," and who fell off a roof and split his head open. But that was later, after Grantville had been torn down to make way for an Interstate 95 bridge, when we called Esther "Streetwalker Morin," and she wore a black motorcycle jacket and yelled obscenities at us as we cruised by in our cars, flipping her the finger.

* * *

A FEW YEARS AGO, I belonged to a health club, where a gaggle of eight to ten-year old boys would shower after swimming lessons. Their high voices echoed off the shower walls—screams, fart-noises, burps, laughs—loud and grating and totally at odds with their frail hairless bodies, bony shoulders, and round stomachs. All I could think of were baby birds squawking in the rain for regurgitated worms.

It's hard to think of myself as having been that age. I know from my earliest, fragmentary memories and from those family stories that help us define who we are ("I remember when you were five and . . .") that I grew up a serious and solitary kid. I liked to crawl into a cabinet next to the chimney in my living room and nestle in the warm darkness, or pull the bed covers over my head when I listened to "Bobby Benson of the B-Bar-B" on the radio. I would wander the woods behind my house for hours and I had a favorite pine tree under which I used to read about Bunny Brown and his sister Sue.

Moving from the two-room primary school just up the street to the third grade in adjoining elementary and junior high schools thrust me into an intimidating world of sixth, seventh, and eighth graders, and because in those days students routinely repeated grades, some of these kids were sixteen and seventeen years old. Freddy Fitts weighed over two hundred pounds, and once twisted my friend Richie Wentworth's arm until he cried. Russell Leavitt, his face ablaze with acne, liked to run after us, growling and waving his arms. Mr. Beal, the eighth grade teacher who patrolled the playground, was an ex-marine who everyone said had killed Japs in World War II. One day I saw him throw my cousin, Bucky

Cleaves, against the side of the school.

Even kids I'd known at the Portland Street School were different here. My old friend Craig Pride now teased me because I was overweight and the only boy he knew who couldn't ride a bicycle. Craig's brother Buzzie and a tall blond kid named Mike Burnham had a gang, most of whom were in the fourth and fifth grades, but because he was Buzzie's brother, Craig and a couple of his friends got to join. Craig bragged about how tough you had to be to belong to Mike 'n Buzzie's gang, and how they threw rotten apples at sissies. I remember running home after school so Mike 'n Buzzie's gang couldn't get me; I stopped reading in the woods behind my house in case they were waiting for me in ambush.

Third grade was about the time I started waking up early on school mornings, staring into the darkness, and shivering with apprehension. I imagined Freddy Fitts breaking my arm; I saw Russell Leavitt throwing me into a mud puddle; I felt rotten apples splattering on my face. I worried the reason I couldn't keep my balance on a bicycle was because I had polio, like Frankie Bell, my cousin with the leg brace.

But as I remember it, Esther Morin changed everything. She was my ticket into Mike 'n Buzzie's gang. The day I copied Craig's gas mask, I joined him and maybe a few of his friends chanting on our way to the playground, "Fart-smeller Morin! Fart-smeller Morin!" Soon afterward, on the afternoon I was scheduled to stay after school to erase blackboards, Craig burst into the classroom as soon as Mrs. Croudis had left for the teachers' room.

"We're getting a gang together for an apple fight with the uptown kids! Big meeting at Mike's house! Let's go!"

Perhaps I'd been dreading this day, afraid Mike 'n Buzzie's gang would be waiting for me when I left school. Now I was being offered a chance to be part of that gang. I threw down the eraser and ran out the door with Craig.

The next morning, Mrs. Croudis bawled me out in front of the class for not finishing my after-school chores—the first time I'd ever gotten in trouble with a teacher. But for the first time, I didn't care. Suddenly, Mrs. Croudis was just a teacher.

I don't remember any apple fight with anybody from uptown, but I know the big kids came to the apple tree behind my house for ammunition. Soon I was showing off my woods and climbing my pine tree with new friends. And through that fall and into the winter, before school or on the way to the playground, anywhere from five to ten of us would surround Esther with our hands over our noses and mouths, hopping up and down like crows and cackling, "Esther is a fart-smeller!" In the halls, we tried to trip her; in class, we targeted her with spit-balls. Sometimes we would wait for Esther after school and run circles around her until she shrieked and swung her long, bony arms. Then we would run off, baying like wolves.

I can't remember if I stopped waking up afraid or not, but I know my school days became a lot happier.

THE CONGREGATION STANDS AND SINGS, and again I'm flipping pages, searching for my place. I don't understand. I'm usually detached from religious services, rating the voices in the choir, smiling to myself when Jesus speaks in a Maine accent, "See? My betrayah is at hand!" Now I'm feeling guilty, not like a man feeling remorse, but like a little boy who has been caught doing something he shouldn't.

Across from me, behind Father Appleyard's square jaw and broad shoulders, Christ stands in a stained glass window, holding the chalice and the host. The morning light shines through red, blue, turquoise, and gold glass, through flowers and foliage, through a bundle of wheat and bunches of grapes. Christ stands, draped in red and white, his right hand raised in blessing. But his face under a helmet of brown hair is bone white, skull-shaped. His deep-set black eyes stare down at me.

The hymn ends. Haloed by sunlight through stained glass, Father Appleyard begins his homily. I tell myself not to trivialize my faith. Poor Esther was a victim, but she was no Christ-symbol. Jesus chose to be a sacrifice for sin; Esther was a poor mentally retarded kid with bad teeth. Besides, sin means you know what you're doing. We were just kids for heaven's sake, and face it, kids are cruel.

Trying not to move my head, I look out of the corner of my eye around the church. Up in the very back pew, complete with bodyguard, the Governor of the State sits under the American flag. Over in the transept, under the Bishop's Window, sits a nationally-known writer and his family. Sitting in the front row, with his hand to his ear, is a retired Bishop. College professors, physicians, and the former chair of the town council are here today. I make a bet with myself that even these success stories have an Esther somewhere in their early chapters.

Then I wonder if someone like Esther actually helps make people successful. Didn't ridiculing her make me stop thinking of myself as a loser—fat, slow, and unpopular? I remember my self-consciousness about being fat; didn't it help to know someone who was ugly? If I was afraid that Freddy Fitts would beat me up, wasn't it reassuring to know there was someone I could hit and no one would care? Wasn't Esther my way to strike back at those morning fears, ridicule them with names like "fart-smeller" and "cootie-lover"? Admit it. Every time Esther screamed and waved her arms like some broken doll because of something I'd said, I felt stronger. Wouldn't we say today that she helped develop "self-esteem"? By the end of the third grade I was riding my bicycle from one end of town to the other. I went on to play baseball and basketball for Mr. Beal. I was the first of my family to go to college and I've been a respected teacher for thirty years. I've just become a church Lay Reader and Chalice Bearer, for heaven's sake. I should look up Esther and thank her.

Jonathan has finished his homily and Margaret is reading those interminable Prayers of the People. The air closes in on me and I'm sweating. If the early Christians had had to wear polyester, the Western world would still be worshipping Jupiter. No, I decide, besides being mocked, Jesus was tortured and executed. Except for perhaps sticking my foot out, I never touched Esther; in fact, I avoided contact for fear of cooties or something. My guilt is misplaced, stupid.

But I find myself glancing uncomfortably up into the black eyes of the stained glass Jesus. I play with my cross. I suddenly remember—remember so clearly I know I'm not making any of it up—Esther sitting against the pale yellow classroom wall, behind a desk that is too small for her, a bare desk, a desk empty of Santa Clauses, hearts, or bunnies, crying silently, her hunched shoulders shaking. And I realize that as often as we picked on her, we ignored her more. She was the last chosen for any team. I doubt that anyone, except perhaps Mary Rollston who took singing lessons and so was also different, ever gave Esther a card or a present at Christmas or Valentine's or Easter.

So which was worse, our loud ridicule or our silent rejection? Haven't people always crucified more often by indifference than by physical torture?

THE OFFERTORY BEGINS. Father Appleyard nods, and I follow him up to the altar.

My brother says that one of the reasons he likes teaching elementary school is that his kids are just beginning to become aware of a larger world around them. Third grade was about the time I sat down with our new 1952 Compton Encyclopedia and first read about aardvarks. Third grade was air-raid drills (down cellar, not under the desk, the town fire whistle blowing a certain set of long and short blasts to let us know an atomic attack was coming), Commies, Joe McCarthy (the first face I remember seeing on television), Korea, polio scares, and my father taking a job for "a goddam Jew."

I learned to divide the world into Us and Them, Red-blooded Americans and Dirty Reds, Good Guys and Bad Guys, Winners and Losers, Mike 'n Buzzie's Gang and Esther Morin. I still tend to see the world that way. How often do I say, "There are two kinds of people in this world . . ."? What am I doing on Palm Sunday but, like my father, separating the successes from the rest of the congregation?

How much did the collective fears of the early 1950s—especially of Communism and the atomic bomb—affect me? I'm not sure, but I expect what I feared most from all those Thems was their derision. Taunting Esther was another way to hide under the covers from Craig Pride's teasing, and I realize that fear of ridicule has always been a driving force in my life. I want to be seen as a figure of importance, whether in the classroom or sitting in a black robe and white surplice on a raised dais in front of the church. Standing beside the altar, I now know that more than the crucifixion, it is the mocking soldiers, the jeering crowd, the thought of being spat upon that bothered me so much when we read the Passion.

It's not a guilty conscience that has made me remember Esther; it's pride, her threat to the image I have of myself as detached and wise. I realize that if there's anyone in this morning's story I should identify with, it's the chief priests and scribes who saw Jesus and his disciples as the Bad Guys. What Peter denies twice is being "one of them," a Galilean, a Loser.

Jonathan raises a round wafer over his head. He snaps it in two, saying, "Christ our Passover is sacrificed for us."

We respond, *"Therefore let us keep the feast."*

And whether I resurrect it by conjecture or by memory, I see Mrs. Croudis taking Esther into the hall outside our classroom. Esther is crying, undoubtedly because of what we, her classmates, have done or what we have not done. Her long nose is red and running, her eyes blood-shot. She is taller than her teacher, stooped over. Mrs. Croudis holds her by the arm. The rest of us sit behind our wooden desks in our plaid shirts and dresses and Buster Brown shoes, hairless and openmouthed, still round with baby fat, feeding on the gaunt and broken body.

...S ISCARIOT CICELY ANGLETON

In upside down silence and nominal blue
I see you in beggar's rags.
Tatterdemalion. Under the shade,
under the shade of a red-bud tree
I hear you breaking the hush, weakly repeating
The True Name in soft repetitive
whine, the True Name, your beggarman's
song blessed by the rustling of leaves
against the luminous bark.

MOVING LUCY VEGA TO THE RESERVATION PAUL LUIKART

afterbirth
in the bed of a pickup.—

a placental tarp is limp, heaped over
a mound of belongings bound by extension cords.—

a life ends in the mess
another begins in the dust.—

Shoved from one life into another
innit, Pima Lucy Vega?

Two truck loads of trash bag possessions,
two trips to the reservation,
and at two in the morning
calling it quits on account of
smelling like horses
tired as the dogs
that sleep in the dust
of your crushed out,
new—dwelling.

You cut the cord, Lucy, first.—
you're oldschool with hooks and ropes
to tie down half your stuff.

Eviction notice,
a midnight move, a
midnight flight is all it takes
to make you a res boy, Joseph.

PAUL LUIKART

Pima Lucy Vega
rolls a smoke—
rushes til the smell of sweat
makes the back of my throat flinch—
takes her son
from the dwelling of the cockroach
to the dwelling of the dogs.—

What is sacred comes:
the eagle feather, the last of the long-haired Pima,
who is copyrighted,
Death blanket, the books
Of course the TV, VCR, stereo.

But a mad dash midnight flight
from the ghetto to the res
doesn't leave a lot of room in the womb
of a white pickup
for more than the spontaneous stuff.

What you see will appall you.

*Dontcha hate it when you're helping somebody
move and you show up and their shit is like,*
        everywhere?

Hi, Paul. Thank you so much.
Hi.
This is my boy Joseph.
Hi, Joseph.
First I needa smoke. So tell me about where you're, where are you from?
Canton, Ohio.
Where?
East.

MOVING LUCY VEGA TO THE RESERVATION

We'll take the TV, VCR, and stereo and the bed.
                                                                                Okay.

You like movies? Who's your favorite actress?
Janeane Garofalo, I guess.
I like her too.

Your life, Pima Lucy—
I stumble onto it, through it in your
living room one night in Phoenix,
the night you're off to the res by midnight
to live with your sister and family and
a shitload of dogs that have Indian names
and are scared of white boys like me.

See this? I note the irony of the situation:
the white man relocating the Indians again . . .
but nothing got me prepared for the mouse lair
you-live-I-should-say-lived-in.
The mountains of books, baby clothes, toys, trash bags,
TV remotes, shelves of mold, and all the other
monuments you've built to desolation.

You see this? I didn't ask for this
and I'm sorry you gotta go Pima Lucy Vega,
but the sheriff is coming tomorrow
and I'm sorry all you got to feed your kid is cans of stuff.

(See this, Lucy Vega, is a white boy from Ohio
scared of what he's doing working in this shit.

You and your boy Joseph gotta head off to the res.

You're a res boy now, Joseph.
Do you even know, Joseph?
Is it getting through to you?)

PAUL LUIKART

A new life, Pima Lucy Vega,
Nothing to do with me, Pima Lucy.

Fuck me.
Fuck me for thinking that. All that.

Lucy, what can I do?
Lucy, what can I do?

A third trip I offer twice but you resist.
Shall I insist?
I want to go home but
I'll insist, Pima Lucy, I'll insist.

Pima Lucy Vega how in the world did you get here?
How can I reach out my white hand
and touch yours: a map of American history.

(All night all we did was slide through conversation
like a snowball gliding across a frozen pond
back east in Canton, Ohio.)

Pima Lucy what can I do?
God sent a white boy from the east
to touch your hand on a desert night.—
Do you ever ask the questions?
Can I ask on your behalf?

God, God.

From the ghetto to the res,
from mice and roaches underfoot
to dogs in dusty shadows
of rotten wood in the corridors
of your   new   home.

Go . . . Do . . . he answers.

MOVING LUCY VEGA TO THE RESERVATION

He answers and I am sent
        along.

Lucy Vega, with your family
and the face of God on your Indian face,
as I finally turn my back and slink away
God bless you on your new life.

ANUNCIATION: TRIPTYCH ANNE M. DOE OVERSTREET

I.
The half moon caught in the orange tree
swaying, a slant husk on the windowsill
facing the Dead Sea. Who can say what
embodies a bowl? What strange messenger
finds his way between limb and the leaf-cast
shadows, filling the hollow clay?

II.
Waking, I begin to shape a vessel large enough
to hold three blood oranges still in their skin.
The lip a curl, the curl where wind no longer follows
the line of a hill, leaps back into the arms of the air.
It may take months to find the particular language
of a wheel, letting the silk slip of clay cover my hands.
All the time filling up, becoming less and less Mary.

III.
My bed is empty, lamp blown Sharp and acidic,
I taste him among the peculiar appetites
of night, taste him like the salt of the sea
miles from this room. Joseph has gone back
to boards and nails, closed to these arms, and I
am empty as a bowl inside. Vast, and humming.

IN THIS PLACE OF GRASS ANNE M. DOE OVERSTREET

We have long known
in this place of grass
and blazing light, of loss
by fire, of death
by flame. We gather the ephemeral
morning flower, catch every
constellation we can
on our tongues
consuming Orion and the Bear
with red sauce and beans
to burn out their cold white taste.

PHOTOGRAPHING THE CROSS CALEE MILAN LEE

We stand in the Kilmeague cemetery. Actually, Jacob stands. I wander, trying to find any patches of warm air on this day passing for an Irish spring. Kilmeague is a tiny village. One butcher. Two pubs. When we slid down into its valley, winding our way along the cheese grater road, the church was glowing in the center. The steeple is three times higher than any other building and the cemetery covers several acres. Who knew there were so many dead people in such a place?

On my first trip to Ireland, I too was entranced by the tombstones. Perhaps it was because I was the one with the camera around my neck. Jacob has offered many times since then to let me photograph the crosses, but I can't see them the way he does. In Don DeLillo's *Mao II*, Brita Nilsson dedicates her life and career to photographing writers. She says, "I frankly have a disease called writers." This is my husband and Ireland's gravestones.

Often, the soft, continuous rain wore away name and date ages ago. Beneath some crosses the family name works its way in, Kavagnah, Byrne, O'Toole, Casey—every surname but our own.

Unlike so many Americans who come to Ireland looking to connect with long lost relatives or explore their roots, we've never talked to another Lee. We may smile every time we pass the Lee River in Cork and once, while trying to buy a vacuum, we heard there was a pocket of Lees living somewhere in our town. We don't come to Ireland to explore our past; visiting cemeteries is a hobby not many of our Irish friends understand.

Now Jacob has the tripod, my least favorite accessory, and dances with it among the graves. He bends down to catch a cross with grass growing in the Celtic circle. He leans to whisper at Mary's cheek.

When it gets too cold I stay in the car, letting him explore another cemetery in a nameless town. In Kilmeague I make a mistake; I brave the cold and wander into the land of the recently buried. Here, fake flowers and stuffed bears crowd the simple, circled crosses. Plaques with photos of the deceased remind me not to step on decaying flesh, only lightly covered by muddy earth. There are too many children. It is easier to linger among the long buried. My husband stands outside of it all. He embraces the dead and the shrines the living have made for them.

What does it mean to photograph a grave? We are not remembering the dead as living, or even as human beings. They are excuses for another replica of the ultimate death. We find beauty in the image. The cracks and overgrowth, all are added character to the cross, a ubiquitous symbol of suffering.

In Chaim Potok's *My Name is Asher Lev*, a young Hasidic boy uses the crucifix as the only art motif that will accurately depict his mother's agony. The cross, despite all of the political and religious ramifications is ultimately an instrument of torture.

I went to 4-H camp in junior high. My bunkmate was Pam, a Mormon girl from La Habra. Besides dancing with a boy to "Black Hole Sun," all I remember about that camp was Pam's question about my cross-shaped lanyard. She didn't understand why I'd wear a murder weapon around my neck. I didn't have a good answer. It was the last time I wore one.

Still, my husband loves the cross. Not in a "wear a gold necklace" or a "buy the neighbors a copy of *The Passion of the Christ*" sort of way. He is hungry for the imagery in the way New Yorkers rush to the parks on the first sunny day of spring.

His churches never had crosses, or if one was required, it was hidden in a corner or floated on a plexi-glass pulpit. Jesus was never hanging.

There seem a million reasons for the bare walls that make up the worship centers of evangelical churches. We can rattle them off without thinking. Christ has risen; why focus on the crucifix? We are not to display graven images. The church should spend its money on helping people, not decoration. These are easy dismissals of centuries of art. We've both seen it in our churches—the unspoken, desperate fear of the past. It may start with a bare wall, but it's only a matter of time before we notice a million different doctrines all shot down in the name of progress. With the rejection of confessions and creeds, common prayers and petitions, the evangelical church has created a place for "personal relationship," but at what cost?

In the States, historic Christianity has often been relegated to seminary students and dusty books, but a crop of "emergent churches" now seeks connection with the past through the transformation and reclamation of ritual. A converted bowling alley displays icons. The coffee shop converts to candles and incense for a Saturday night service. A few young American churches are trying to recreate a connection with a past that may have never existed in their town.

This is not a problem in Ireland. The religious past is ever present, threatening to halt construction on motorways and tangle debates about everything from architecture to social welfare. It is impossible to live a normal life without running into ancient Christian ruins. That is, until you step into an evangelical church.

In one warehouse-turned-church building, each wall displays a Thomas Kincaid landscape. Plastic chairs face a pulpit with a felt panel reading "Holy Spirit." There is no crucifix, nothing that resembles the interior of the Catholic Church down the street. There are plenty of Christians who would argue that an evangelical presence should stand in striking contrast to Catholicism, both aesthetically and theologically. Still, American visitors have had difficulty differentiating this place from any other little evangelical church in the Midwest. I suppose there is nothing wrong with this expression of Christianity but the digital projector seems so out of place in a country famed for illuminated manuscripts.

Pastors across the island insist they are creating a "uniquely Irish" evangelical church through their emphasis on community and free expression. Even evangelical churches that have graduated from rental hotel conference rooms to their own buildings have chosen to eschew traditional architecture and decoration for a more modern approach. They want to evangelize their community by defining themselves, not with the religion of the church of their fathers, but with seeker-sensitive methods and a friendly atmosphere.

Yet beneath all the rhetoric of creating a "uniquely Irish" evangelical church, I feel more connected to centuries of Irish Christians in a graveyard than a contemporary sanctuary. American evangelicals overflowing with good intentions have sent missionaries, teachers and plenty of money to try and win back the "land of saints and scholars." As a result, the infant evangelical movement is growing and offering a positive religious alternative to a country saturated by the same scandals that have haunted the American priesthood. The flip side is a creation of mini-American churches where the only difference is the way "worship centre" is spelled. In trying to change the future of Ireland, the evangelical church is forgetting its past.

WE DRIVE TO MEET AN EVANGELICAL PASTOR in a tiny town outside of Galway. He gives us directions saying, "turn at the T-junction." We, of course, miss the mysterious and unmarked junction and end up in the car park for the local Catholic Church. Twenty minutes later, the pastor drives up to lead us to his home. He points across the street; we just missed our turn. We're not sure why he didn't use the towering steeple to direct us.

AS AN AMERICAN IN IRELAND, I am already walking on eggshells. The Irish are a fiercely independent people, unwilling to accept conquerors, no matter the version of English they speak. They are not fans of the Iraq war, nor do they see the US as being a perfect, Christian nation. The Irish church is no different. In each town we are greeted with hospitality, but friendship only comes after we make it clear we have no interest in telling the pastor how to run his church.

In some ways, Jacob and I are no different than the Americans who have come before; we want to help the Irish church grow. Neither of us grew up Catholic, nor do we fully understand what it means to live as a member of the religious minority. After logging thousands of miles in our Nissan Micro, we are still trying to understand how a country that once supplied the world's priests is moving beyond its history and beyond the cross.

As nationwide church attendance continues to decrease and new social problems like teen suicide and drug abuse sweep the country, my husband and I have committed to finding Americans who are willing to help the young evangelical presence spread. Sometimes we cringe when we walk into a church and can't tell which country we are in. In our emerging, postmodern little minds, we want to hold services in Quin Abbey, even if it means freezing because there is no roof. It seems strange that we've visited more of Ireland's religious sites than the local pastors.

Then we remember that we are not Irish. Even if our last name allows our future children to make a shamrock for a family tree, we are Americans and will always think that way. When I am bitterly honest, I know I came to Ireland projecting all of my hopes of what church should look like onto this developing church. It is not my place, nor my responsibility, to guide the aesthetic decisions of Irish evangelicals.

Every once in a while, I still borrow the camera. I look through the viewfinder at a stone cross, weathered and covered in ivy. It's not going anywhere. I snap a photo and hand the camera back. My husband takes another picture of the same cross at a different angle. We will always have different perspectives. As the evangelical church adapts with the seasons, it is like the moss on the stone. Christ and the cross remain central, the way it looks to the outside only changes. For some, only mass is the way to see a crucifix. For others, the sermon behind a plexi-glass pulpit is sufficient. We connect to the Christians of Ireland in graveyards; perhaps our neighbors will one day do so in a tiny, evangelical church.

FLOTSAM JEFF P. JONES

From merging headwaters
of streams colder,
home of the shadowy
freestone river
where the seasons rise and fall
and line the boulders,

where if rushing or slow
the current
depends on snow
and distant peaks,

where, unhinged,
sometimes the sun drops
beneath scree
and blacker scores
the ash-black soil
in shaded runnels;

ambered in colorless current,
past ponderosas,
past firs, and broad, red cedars,

through early morning,
a duck carcass floats,
the stomach flashing pale,
pale mirroring clouds,
tumbling as if to say there's nothing
left to hide—

and swiftly passes, silent, while
two fishermen pause
to see if a beak will break
the surface and breathe.

EL ORACION DE LA CIUDAD HEATHER MICHELLE STEWART

The mountains, olive colored mounds
of clay God has pressed
his knuckles into—their song
is the breeze whirling around me
like quiet meringues.

From the clouds, brown and green
triangles and squares fit together
like a broken mosaic. Stone walls
hold up the inner city, barbed wires,
and glass that keep the sky
from falling and poor men stealing
black bananas.

The crooked footsteps of girls, heavy with the sun,
are carrying tortillas, smoke rising, pieces
of a puzzle, unsolved. In the valley, children
wash clothes on rocks where
there used to be a river. Women beat rugs
from balconies, the dust
falls, the sky darkens.

We sit with the people under their tin
roofs, wipe sweat from our straining muscles
that have hammered hope into each board.
One day these walls of Jericho
will fall, and the sunset will mean
something beautiful, even when we're not
here handing out our hearts.
Tonight as we sing from the roof tops,

EL ORACION DE LA CIUDAD

orange lights in the distance are
burning out: goodnight Gustavo,
David, Carlos, y Rachel, wherever
you are. There is a prayer
for a better sunrise written
in the stars for all of us.

A MIRACLE FOR MARTY LOIS BARLIANT

BECCA HADN'T DRESSED FOR A MIRACLE. No one else in the crowd starting up the hill was wearing a pastel sun dress or spaghetti sandals. The prospect of the slippery stones up the steep street to the chapel irked her, but she understood her obligation. In Mexico City on her one free day, she could be sitting at a sidewalk café drinking a chocolaté before checking out the little shops with lazy fans spreading warm air over the tooled leather purses, ceramic plates with navy blue flowers and sun-faced mugs, or designer knock-offs marked half-price, but Marty had lymphoma, and Becca had agreed to make the trek to this little church.

Eleven o'clock and sweat ran down between her shoulder blades to the loose belt around her waist. The sun's reflection off whitewashed buildings seared her eyes. Even the geraniums on the balconies stung like pepper. Donkeys pulled carts painted in bright reds, yellows, blues, greens, and oranges toward the church. They didn't stop while urinating bubbling streams that puddled in the crevices between the stones. Becca grinned, barely, at Javier, the concierge from the Hotel de la Vista Regal who had volunteered to shepherd her through the ordeal. Chickens pecked between the stones for bits of gossip, clucking their disgust at the state of the world. Goats, bleating, tried to shake off the tinkling bells from around their necks. Pigs grunted, nosing for scraps. The dogs had succumbed to the heat and lay on their sides, their legs straight out in front them. Only a fool would have expected serenity on a religious excursion. Javier put out his hand to keep her from stepping in chicken droppings. He went along to pray so that his wife would have a baby.

Javier had promised her the local Mariachi bands would play their best tunes in the hope of being hired for a party. Their silver spangles and the embroidery on their satin and velvet suits jarred Becca more than the blasts of their trumpets and the beat of their guitars. The animals' clucks, bleats, and grunts along with the blare of the bands annihilated any sense of the divine.

Marty would have loved the mix of carnival and farm life. Trudging up the hill with Javier would have been an adventure for her. But she was back in Chicago in a hospital bed.

Becca stopped to look up to *La Capilla de Santa Lucera*, picturing her sister, trying to believe that this pilgrimage would help Marty get better. Steps had been chiseled into the rock. People pushed wheelchairs and others on their knees crept up this path, praying their way to the chapel. The prospect of crowding into that small sanctuary with all the sick and crippled crumpled what little was left of Becca's hope for Marty's recovery. A young man passing them coughed and spit his phlegm on the ground, and now every stone stuck to the sole of Becca's sandals. No wonder the vendors kept sweeping the road with wet brooms. Becca arched her back and stared up. On a dome too large for the chapel, a stark black cross punctuated the blue sky.

Marty was the religious one; she had been since they were little. She started attending Sunday school on her own after their grandmother died. No one discouraged Marty, but Becca and her mother didn't mean it when they told her to put in a good word for them, and they rolled their eyes at one another when Marty admitted that she had prayed for them. After she got caught up in Russian Orthodoxy and went to religious retreats instead of vacationing with them in Cancun, they began to have serious conversations about saving her from herself. Becca and their mother believed what made sense, condoned what helped society, and scoffed at what smacked of superstition. Then, the year after the twins graduated from college, their mother's breast cancer returned, and Marty immediately planned a trip to France with a stop at Lourdes. She brought back a vial of healing water.

Their mother shrugged at Becca. "It can't hurt."

After Marty left, Becca stayed at the hospital and held her mom's hand. The bed was cranked up so she could see a terrace garden outside. A bed of red tulips blazed in the afternoon light. "Are you going to drink it or rub it on?" she asked. Her mother held it up to the light. It looked gray.

"I'm going to hold it." Her mother pondered the tulips and then smiled at Becca. "A miracle would be good."

The biopsies came back clean, and follow-up examinations for ten years running indicated that Becca's mother was cancer free. She never said that the holy water made a difference, but Becca knew she credited the healing to Marty's trip.

Then, six months ago, Marty was diagnosed with cancer of the lymph nodes. The surgery at Northwestern had been successful. "What they mean," she said, as she sucked small pieces of ice Becca spooned into her parched mouth, "is that I have a little longer to hope they'll quit coming in here at 6 a.m. to check my vital signs." Flecks of skin sloughed off her gums and around the edges of her mouth. Becca watched trickles from the melting ice creep into cracks in her tongue and lips. She stayed late into the night so the ice could relieve the dryness.

The Monday before leaving for the business trip to Mexico City, Becca told Marty she couldn't visit for a week. Marty wished she could go to Manzanilla again.

Becca rubbed cream on the dry skin of Marty's arms, hands, legs, and feet. The skin stretched across her forehead had a ivory sheen with clearly visible veins, cold as stone to Becca's fingers.

"About a hundred miles south of Mexico City, there's a church." Marty closed her eyes as if to picture it. "It's similar to Lourdes—without the grotto." She opened her eyes and grinned at Becca. "A light surrounds the chapel; it cures people." She held two fingers of Becca's hand like a child might. "It was out of the way. I guess I should have gone." She almost laughed—a dry, hacking cough.

"I'll go." The words came out by themselves. Becca didn't mean them, but once they were out, she couldn't take them back.

"I'm not suggesting you go." Marty turned to look out the window, and Becca could tell that she really hadn't meant for her to volunteer. Marty knew Becca didn't believe in miracles; her awareness was in her focus on the striated wall opposite her hospital window. Marty was dying, and the nurses couldn't be bothered to bring her fresh ice cubes.

"You did it for Mom."

"It's okay, Becca. I meant the church is supposed to be worth the trip."

"I know. I understand. I'll go."

Marty's head had rolled back on the pillow and she had closed her eyes. "So do you think the Cubs will let Sosa go?"

The sky had been intensely blue that day, though Becca only saw it because she stood next to the window and could look straight up. She hated the thought that Marty only saw beige stone walls and the bouquets of drooping daisies with a Mylar happy face balloons, oppressively fragrant star lilies stuck in carnations and snapdragons, and planters with waxy green plastic-looking leaves crowded between the boxes of tissue and opened but not consumed cans of protein drink stuck with giraffe neck flexible straws.

On the path up the hill to the church, men and women hawked pastries in the shape of the chapel, squeezed fresh lemons, limes, and oranges, and rearranged rosaries, lace head coverings, jewelry, dishes, bottled water, sun glasses, Flamenco Barbie dolls, and Ken dolls dressed like Elvis. Tapes and CDs blasted hip hop and sacred music, an alternative to the mariachi bands. A woman yelled out that Javier should buy his girlfriend a hot tortilla. He waved her off and shook his head with disgust at her assumption about Becca. She wasn't the only tourist among those trudging single-mindedly toward the church, but she was the only one in a raspberry-pink knee-length dress. Most of the women had mantillas around their shoulders to cover their heads inside the chapel. Becca thought about buying one, but Javier told her not to worry about it. "God doesn't care about those things."

Becca didn't ask how Javier knew what matters to God. Marty would say the same thing.

"So, what's supposed to happen? What do I do exactly?" Some women were kneeling outside the church.

"You don't do anything. You go in and pray for the person you love. You buy a candle and light it and put it in front of the altar." Javier explained that at noon the midsummer sun enters directly in through a skylight in the rafters and reflects off the gold of the saint's tomb. "That light is God's presence right here in Santa Lucera." His gesture of opening his palms upward suggested it was all up to the divine and it didn't really matter what Becca did.

Becca didn't think God should pick one place over another or make people crawl half a mile up a hill to be healed. "People have to come for the summer solstice or no miracles take place?"

"No, no, Senora!" Javier shook his head at her question. He flapped his hand for her to go on up the last flight of stairs. "People are healed all year round. Miracles happen all the time. You can read the stories. Inside are plenty of newspaper clippings nailed to the door and pillars."

They reached the top and went inside. Thick walls kept the air cool and still. The only opening was the skylight above the altar. Darkness hung in the air as Becca looked away from the altar and the place of the tomb. Heavy curtains caught the street noises and stopped the light from the vestibule, while inside votive candles flickered on the altar railing, davening with every person's entry. As her eyes adjusted to the darkness, she heard the rustle of other petitioners, their murmurs, quiet weeping, wheezing, coughing, and the squeak of wheelchairs and walkers. In the chapel's rectangular space, only slightly longer than wide, the saint was buried in front of a simple altar at the north end. St. Lucera's husband had built the church to honor his wife and the work she had done to help the poor. It was the kind of story Marty liked.

The crowd surging into the sanctuary separated Becca from Javier, but she didn't mind. She had decided to see the gold reflect the sun at its highest point and stepped in front of people on crutches, maneuvered around a blind man without touching his cane, and whispered "Escusame," to three women leaning together, their lips fingering prayers as their rosaries passed through their hands. Two priests walked through the crowd, swinging censors of incense and keeping pathways clear so people could place their candles on the rail in front of the altar and file back leaving space for others. The older one looked like a Mexican Clint Eastwood. The younger could have modeled for El Greco or Picasso during his blue period.

Becca was stopped short behind an old man guiding his wife, each step a matter of inches, to the altar. In his shiny brown suit that hung from his shoulders, despite the slow progress, he seemed proud of his wife in her black silk dress that sagged to the floor in the front. Their smell of dried urine and dusty talcum powder forced Becca to hold her breath except for quick gasps as she tried to get around them. For the old guy, Becca wished that the woman, with her drawn-out moans, would feel better. Becca wished Marty were there to pray for the couple. She wished Marty were there for herself.

A man with shoulder-length greasy black hair in an electric blue blazer kept Becca from edging around the couple. He carried a wheezing kid wrapped in blankets; each breath a congested draw of the incensed air. The man might have been twenty-five; his sun-browned face had deep lines down his cheeks, a grim tight-lipped mouth, and eyes focused on the area in front of the altar. Though she knew better, Becca peered over his shoulder at the child's face. Gray and still, it looked dead. A teenager in a shirt with a spangled Marilyn Monroe face had budged between them. "M'hijo," she said to the man who turned so his wife could wipe the baby's face with a Wet One. Becca squeezed herself around them in time for a woman in an yellow Jill St. John suit to push a wheel chair over Becca's toes. Before Becca could give her a piece of her mind, the woman, wrapped in the scent of a citrus-flower, whispered "Excusame." Tears tracked the woman's powdered cheeks. Her emaciated sister or friend in black Armani held a prayerbook.

Becca squirmed at the thought of being a usurper. She tried to fit words from some childhood prayer together, and then the wake of the wheelchair sucked her into the row of people closest to the altar. If only Marty were there with her. Javier was. Right next to her, against the velvet swag protecting the altar area, he gazed up at the crucifix above the altar, as he crossed himself repeatedly, lifting his medallion of the Virgin of Guadalupe to his lips. Becca let a couple of people squeeze between her and Javier so he wouldn't feel she was honing in on his prayer. She hoped the woman in the Armani and the kid in the blanket would get better; she wanted that and she wanted Marty to get well, but the words she put together seemed too forced to be a prayer. She tried thinking "Amen" and hoping that Marty's God would apply it to the prayers of all the sick.

Becca tried to see the tomb, but the swags kept her back. She wasn't going to let a band of velvet keep her from her mission for the day. If Marty couldn't be there, at least Becca could tell her about the tomb at the bottom of the steps. The dome had been designed for sunshine to illuminate the gold lid of the coffin and reflect back up on the people in the immediate area. Becca was going to absorb that reflection for Marty. She had to be in the line of light for the miracle to happen. Becca understood the magic of a place like Disney World: you know it's not real, but you believe it while you're there, and she was going to do her best for Marty.

Becca put her hand on the swag, and the Clint Eastwood priest glanced over, but when she played the tourist looking at the altar, the sky light, the Jill St. John with the wheelchair, he turned away. Waiting until the sun was directly above St. Lucera's tomb with its radiance spread on every worshiper's face or bowed head, Becca unhooked the nearest swag, ran down the first few steps, and leaned over to look at the saint's tomb. The crowd gasped its disapproval. She didn't care. She had to be in the exact spot of the miracle itself. She looked down at a gold plate with a glowing relief of the pious woman. According to the figure, Santa Lucera was short with her hair parted in the middle, and a broad face like the women Diego Rivera painted. Though disappointed, Becca didn't have time to study the woman's effigy because a blast of sun on the polished surface reflected back, blinding her. The brightness surprised her, and she slipped, her seat on the top step, her elbow stopping her from hitting her head on the stone floor. The murmur of the crowd was like a storm roaring over her, but, as if in the sky, Santa Lucera's face glowed from the ceiling. It wasn't the peasant woman on the sarcophagus, but the face of a regal woman wearing a mantilla. Visions of the saint giving food to the hungry, clothes to the poor, medicine to the sick, and comfort to the imprisoned lit panels around the dome. The saint's husband stood in the background of each, amazed at his wife's kindness as if her gracious acts of piety imbued him with God's love. Becca couldn't speak, but she pointed upward. She wanted all of them to see the saint in beautiful, radiant light. If only Marty could see this miracle.

The young priest, his hair flaming out like dark wings above his black cassock, had run down to pull her away from the holy spot. He looked up instead, and slowly sat down next to her, his body shaking. "Mire, Mire. Arriba, arriba." He pointed to the ceiling of the dome. "La santa! Santa Lucera!" His face glowed with the light shining through the alabaster panels.

The roar filling the dome had changed to an a-a-a-h as if a choir master toned their pitch, each person astounded by the glow of the ceiling from the diffused circle of sunlight. The space between the rafters and the thin alabaster slabs filled the dull yellowed stone with the sun's energy. At the very top, she smiled down at them, her eyes and smile beaming with beauty and charity. Then the light faded and a stillness filled the chapel.

Becca shuddered at the sudden dimming of the light.

The priest rose and helped her to her feet. The blood had drained from his face, but his eyes radiated the light from the saint. He babbled in Spanish as he put his arm around her to guide her up the steps. She tried to tell him she was all right, but no words came out.

The alabaster panes had faded to flat surfaces of old yellow. Becca's eyes lost focus in the shadowy light. The man with the child blended into a pillar. The women connected by the wheel chair fused together. Becca thought her eyes would adjust, but, when she opened them, the darkness had intensified.

Leading Becca to a pew, the priest sat down next to her, and she smelled again the faint salt sour odor of people.

She had forgotten to pray for Marty's recovery.

Javier came over, skittish of her.

Becca looked back at the ceiling and saw the faint outline of the scenes from the saint's life still there. They were intaglio images lit from between the outer dome and the tiles by the direct sunlight. Without the sun's direct light, they looked like naturally occurring swirls in alabaster. It was an architect's trick.

Becca felt sorry for all the people who had come, for the old couple, the young father, the girl with the photo, the Jill St. John lady. She felt sorry for Javier. She felt worst of all for Marty. A beautiful light had duped all of them. It was practically impossible not to see that saint as alive, but it wasn't a miracle.

The people in the chapel moved aside for Javier to steer Becca past. Others streamed in; word had gotten out that an American had seen a vision.

In the vestibule, the old man in the brown suit stood next to his wife sitting on a bench.

His wife whispered, "Gracias a Dios por la luz." She reached out a arthritic hand toward Becca.

"Muchas gracias, senorita!"

"Vaya con Dios." Javier knew the words Becca needed.

The miracle they thought took place was architecture and timing. She wouldn't tell that to Marty back in the oncology unit, her head a weight on the pillow.

Outside, The sun blinded them. Javier took a deep breath and stood there, his head tilted toward the light. He had the flat eyes and nose of the Aztec gods.

"Amazing." He shook his head in disbelief.

"Yeah." Becca had no problem admitting that what she had seen amazed her. The light in the chapel had been spectacular even without seeing the saint's glowing face, but, when it lit the carved face from within, that was a once in a lifetime experience.

The light had been real. The scenes had been beautiful. If there was a miracle, it was that she had seen them. If she hadn't fallen, nobody would have looked up. That had to be some kind of miracle.

Becca shook her head to clear the confusion she felt. "My sister's really sick."

"She'll get well now."

"She's really sick."

"Exactemente. She'll get well."

"It wasn't a miracle, you know."

He squinted and stared at her before looking away at the mountains on the horizon.

She waited for him to say something. "It's the light. It's a builder's trick."

He shook his head; he didn't want to hear any more.

"There are two domes and when the light…"

"You don't understand miracles." He bolted ahead and scrambled down the steps. At the first landing, he waited for her to catch up.

They passed the red geraniums and the hens scratching in the dust. The woman was still frying tortillas in front of a blue door surrounded by red, yellow, and pink hibiscus while her children played in the street. At the foot of the slope, Javier stopped to buy a plastic model of Mickey Mouse sporting a serape. "For my son," he told Becca. The owner of the stand kept winding up the dolls so they would walk in around in tiny circles throwing their white gloved hands up in the air while the man's parrot, with one foot tied to a string, hopped along the fence screeching, "Ayudame, Ayudame!" Sick as she was, Marty would have loved it. Becca bought an ever-hopeful Mickey to take back.

AN INTRODUCTION TO OUR AUTHORS

CICELY ANGLETON
FOR JUDAS ISCARIOT
Poetry

Cicely Angleton was born in Duluth Minnesota, 1922, brought up in Tucson, AZ, and graduated Vassar College, PhD at Catholic University of America in medieval studies. She has studied at the Writer's Center, Bethesda, MD for many years. Her publications include *A Cave of Overwhelming*, a collection of poems, *Delos, Poetry, Passager*. She won the Passager contest in 2005 and has given several readings in the Washington/Virginia area. She was married to James Angleton, who went on to be with the Lord in 1987, has three children and two grandchildren, and currently resides in Great Falls, Virginia.

LOIS BARLIANT
A MIRACLE FOR MARTY
Fiction

Lois Barliant worked in advertising and taught high school English before working full-time on writing. She has had stories and essays published in *The Clothesline Review*, *The Chicago Quarterly Review*, *The Rambunctious Review*, *Out of Line*, and *Heartlands, a Magazine of Midwest Life and Art*, and she is working on a novel. She also works as an editor for the *Chicago Quarterly Review*. She was born in Colorado but has lived most of her life in Chicago.

J. BRISBIN
SINS OF THE FATHERS
Editor's Choice for Fiction

J. Brisbin lives in rural southwest Missouri with his wife and five children. He is currently a non-traditional student in the Creative Writing program at an area university. His other short fiction has appeared in *The Cow Creek Review*. He's currently knee-deep in his first novel about a rural Arkansas town in the 1920's, a roaming revival preacher, bootleggers, and a boy named Samuel. His tastes are unpredictably eclectic and he has recently begun trolling thrift shops for vintage suits from the 1930's and '40s. He maintains an Art Deco-themed blog at http://jbrisbin.com.

SCOTT CAIRNS
AND WHY THEOLOGY
Poetry

Scott Cairns is the author of six collections of poetry, most recently, *Compass of Affection*. His works have been anthologized in *Best American Spiritual Writing*, *American Religious Poems*, *Upholding Mystery*, *Shadow & Light*, and elsewhere. His poetry has appeared in *The Atlantic Monthly*, *The Paris Review*, *The New Republic*, *Poetry*, *Image*, *Spiritus*, *Tiferet*, etc. He is Professor of English and Director of Creative Writing at University of Missouri. He received a Guggenheim Fellowship in 2006. His spiritual memoir, *Short Trip to the Edge*, and his verse adaptations and translations, *Love's Immensity: Mystics on the Endless Life*, both appeared in 2007.

AUTHOR BIOS

ANN CEFOLA
BOYS OF IONA PREP
ST. AGNES, PINK SLIPPED
Poetry

Ann Cefola is the author of *Sugaring* (Dancing Girl Press, 2007) and translator of Hélène Sanguinetti's *Hence this cradle* (Seismicity Editions, 2007). Ann is a 2007 Witter Bynner Poetry Translation Fellow and recipient of the 2001 Robert Penn Warren Award judged by John Ashbery. In addition to *Confrontation* and *Natural Bridge*, her work has appeared in *Hunger Enough* (Pudding House, 2004) and *Off the Cuffs* (Soft Skull, 2003). Ann holds an MFA in Poetry from Sarah Lawrence College and works as a creative strategist with her own company, Jumpstart (jumpstartnow.net). She and her husband, Michael, live in the New York suburbs.

CHRISTOPHER ESSEX
SAINTS OF COLORADO
Fiction

Christopher Essex received an MFA in Creative Writing from Indiana University, where he was a Hemingway Fellow and served as fiction editor at the Indiana Review. He earned my bachelor's degree in English from the University of Colorado-Boulder, where he worked on the staff of Rolling Stock and Walkabout magazines. He has had short stories published in *The Portland Review*, *Sou'wester*, *Pearl*, *Fugue*, *The MacGuffin*, *Whiskey Island*, *Blue Mesa Review*, *Crescent Review*, *Flying Island*, *Bathtub Gin*, and other literary magazines. Christopher passed away on April 17, 2007. He will be sorely missed by his friends and family.

MAUREEN TOLMAN FLANNERY
SOMETIMES THE PLAGUES ARE SCHEDULED
SECOND WHITSUN
Editor's Choice for Poetry

Maureen Tolman Flannery's latest books are *Ancestors in the Landscape: Poems of a Rancher's Daughter* and *A Fine Line*. Although she grew up in a Wyoming sheep ranch family, Maureen and her actor husband Dan have raised their four children in Chicago. Her work has appeared in forty anthologies and over a hundred literary reviews, recently including *Birmingham Poetry Review*, *Xavier Review*, *Calyx*, *Pedestal*, *Atlanta Review*, *Language and Culture*, and *North American Review*.

S. JASON FRALEY
SHE CAN'T REMEMBER SOCRATES
BECAUSE THERE IS NO EASY ANSWER
Poetry

Jason Fraley works at an investment firm in West Virginia and is almost finished (thankfully!) with his MBA. His wife and cat see him occasionally. He has appeared or is forthcoming in *Forklift Ohio*, *42opus*, *The Hat*, *Pebble Lake Review*, *Caketrain*, and *No Tell Motel*.

DEANNA HERSHISER
AN OVERTURE'S TURN
Editor's Choice for Creative Nonfiction

Now that her two children are fairly well grown, Deanna Hershiser writes most days in Eugene, Oregon. Her articles have appeared in several magazines and the local newspaper. She has taught continuing education classes at Lane Community College, and she's been known to pet-sit, package toothpaste in a friend's warehouse, and donate plasma. Lately she tries to figure out blogging at http://storieshappen.blogspot.com. Her engineer husband encourages her to put ads on her site so they can pay for college tuition.

DON HOESEL
GOODBYE SOPHIE
Winner
Faith * In * Fiction Daily Sacrament Contest

Don Hoesel lives in Spring Hill, TN with his wife and two children. He is the author of five novels, and has just started work on his sixth, *Comedy Club*, which he hopes will be the one that finally finds a home.

JEFF P. JONES
FLOTSAM
Poetry

Jeff P. Jones's work has won the Wabash Prize in Fiction, the Lamar York Prize in Nonfiction, and the Hackney National Short Story Award. He has work in or forthcoming from *Gulf Coast*, *Puerto del Sol*, *Sycamore Review*, *Hawai'i Pacific Review*, *Mississippi Review*, and elsewhere. He lives and writes on the Palouse in northern Idaho.

JILL KANDEL
DILL
Creative Nonfiction

Jill Kandel lived on the banks of the Luangingwa River in Zambia for six years. Later she lived in western Indonesia, Reading England, and in her husband's native Netherlands. After ten years of living abroad she returned to the United States. She currently lives with her husband and four children in northern Minnesota. She was awarded the Carol Bly Creative Nonfiction Award from Bemidji State University. She has been published in *Minnesota Literature*, *North Country*, and *Dust & Fire*. Jill has a BS, RN degree which she seldom uses since creative nonfiction has devoured her life.

DEBRA KAUFMAN
FEAST DAY OF ST. URSULA
EASTER
APRIL FOOLS
GRACE
Poetry

Debra Kaufman is a poet and playwright who lives in Mebane, North Carolina. She is the author of two chapbooks: *Family of Strangers* and *Still Life Burning*, and the collection *A Certain Light*. Her poems have appeared in many literary magazines and several anthologies, and her plays and monologues have been produced throughout North Carolina and in California.

RENEE RONIKA KLUG
WE THE PEOPLE OF BARBIE
Creative Nonfiction

Renee Ronika Klug spends semesters and summers teaching English at the college level, and holidays in Arizona, where she is from; in New York, where her newlywed husband is from; or in other countries, where she wishes she were from. She prefers the ocean over dry land but enjoys the strenuous hike, particularly in her newest home—Colorado. Renee has a bachelor's degree in English from Biola University and a Master of Fine Arts degree in creative writing from Southampton College.

AUTHOR BIOS

CALEE M. LEE
PHOTOGRAPHING THE CROSS
Creative Nonfiction

Calee M. Lee studied screenwriting at New York University but now focuses her energies on the world of nonfiction. She lives in Southern California with her husband and is thrilled to have let her exhausted passport take a well-deserved rest in favor of raising her newborn daughter. "Photographing the Cross" is from her latest project—a collection of essays about Suburban Pilgrims.

PAUL LUIKART
MOVING LUCY VEGA TO THE RESERVATION
Poetry

Paul Luikart lives in Chicago with his wonderful wife Emily. During the day he works as a case manager for a ministry that assists homeless men and women. He has a BA in English–creative writing from Miami University in Oxford, Ohio and his poetry has appeared in Miami's literary magazine *Inklings* as well as in small publications like *VOiCE* and *The Lucid Stone*. He is currently working on his first collection of short stories.

ALYS MATTHEWS
DANCES WITH OLIVIA
Creative Nonfiction

Alys Matthews is a high school senior in the small town of Gloucester, Virginia. She lives with her mother and two sisters, and is active in her youth group and annual mission trips with the Rappahannock District Youth Choir, a traveling choral group. Writing has been her lifelong passion, and she hopes to major in English and pursue a writing career. Her biggest priorities are family, friends, and trying to see a little piece of God in everything. This is her first publication.

CHRISTOPHER MULROONEY
LETTER TO THE CHURCHES
Poetry

Christopher Mulrooney has written poems and translations in *Pusteblume*, *The Tusculum Review*, *Cake*, *Marginalia*, and *Santa Fe Literary Review*, and criticism in *Elimae*, *Blue Fifth Review*, and *Parameter*.

GREGORY O'NEILL
STANDARD AND DISTINCT THINGS
Poetry

Gregory O'Neill resides in Washington State. His poetry has most recently appeared in *Lily Literary Journal*, *The Dande Review*, *Triplopia*, *The Adroitly Placed Word* Audio Poetry Project (johnvick.org), and *The Furnace Review*. Upcoming in *Wolf Moon Journal Press*, *Tryst Poetry Journal*, and *The Penwood Literary Review*. His chapbook, *Higher Toward Lumen* is being compiled for publishing. The author would recommend Angus Fletcher's *New Theory For American Poety*.

ANNE M. DOE OVERSTREET
ANNUNCIATION
IN THIS PLACE OF GRASS
Poetry

Anne M. Doe Overstreet lives just shy of Seattle, works as a free-lance editor, and runs a small gardening business. If she's not pulling a weed, she's got her nose in a book, or, okay, stereotypically, a cup of coffee. A long-standing member of the Meridian Poets' group and a Soapstone Writing Residency recipient, her work has appeared in publications such as *DMQ Review*, *Cranky*, *Northwest Mirror*, *Talking River Review*, and *TheMatthewsHouseProject.com*. Her most recent poetic adventure was opening a meeting of Seattle's Public Safety, Civil Rights, & Arts Committee with a piece about grandmothers and high heels.

ANGIE POOLE
THE MATING HABITS OF LIZARDS
Runner Up
Faith * In * Fiction Daily Sacrament Contest

Angie Poole, CPA counts beans in Texas Forest Country. She insists there is no true distinction between left brain/right brain because Story resides in between. Her fishtales can be found at www.angiepoole.blogspot.com.

ELLEN MORRIS PREWITT
JESUS CALLED
Fiction

Ellen Morris Prewitt lives with her husband and two Yorkies in Memphis. Her fiction has appeared in *Image*, *Southern Hum*, *Arkansas Review*, *Eureka Literary Magazine*, *Gulf Coast Literary Journal*, *Peralta Press*, and elsewhere. Excerpts from her memoir have been in *Alaska Quarterly Review*, *North Dakota Quarterly*, and *River Teeth*. Her first novel was a semi-finalist in the James Jones First Novel Competition, 2005. A short story received Special Mention in the *Pushcart Prize XXXI: Best of the Small Presses*, 2007. She makes religious objects from broken and found objects, a book on which is in the works.

HEATHER MICHELLE STEWART
EL ORACION DE LA CIUDAD
Poetry

Heather Stewart is a writer at Blake School of the Arts and captain of the Varsity Swim and Soccer Team. She is involved in her youth group and annual mission trips to Honduras. She has been published in the literary magazine *Synapse*, *Celebration of Young Poets*, the *Hillsborough County Teachers of English Annual Contest Anthology*, and *Who's Who Among High School Students*. She has been a National English Merit Award Winner in 2005 and 2006. She recently received an Honorable Mention in Poetry from the National Foundation for the Advancement of the Arts. She is attending Lipscomb University in Nashville, Tennessee in 2007.

MARIANNE TAYLOR
LAMENT IN A COUNTRY GRAVEYARD
Poetry

Marianne Taylor is a Professor of English at Kirkwood Community College where she teaches literature and creative writing. She has been the recipient of the Allen Ginsberg Award and the Helen A. Quade Memorial Writer's Award; and her manuscript, *Salt Water, Iowa*, has been a finalist for the John Ciardi Prize for Poetry, the Richard Snyder Memorial Poetry Prize, and the Winnow Press Open Book Award. Her work has been published widely in national journals such as *Nimrod International Journal*, *North America Review*, *Alaska Quarterly Review*, *Connecticut Review*, and *Rosebud*. She lives in the small town of Mount Vernon, IA, with her husband and four sons.

AUTHOR BIOS

J. MARCUS WEEKLEY
MISS SWEETY'S ROCK-OLA MACHINE
Fiction

J. Marcus Weekley has struggled and rested in his relationship with God for the past sixteen years; it's like a marriage on the rocks, but they're still married. His writing bears out this relationship, sometimes directly, sometimes under the surface. Marcus' writing has appeared in *Quick Fiction*, *The Iowa Review*, *Margin*, *Theives Jargon*, *Poetry International*, and *Poetry Salzburg Review*, among other places. Marcus is the author of four books, including *something about*, *dawn breaks*, and *a tree isn't a tree*, each available at www.lulu.com/whynottryitagain (and *The Collaborative Texas Dance Halls: a Two-step Circuit*, forthcoming from Texas Tech University Press, Fall 2007). His artistic heroes include George Herbert, Harry Callahan, Flannery O'Connor, Stephen King, Anne Sexton, Ben Neihart, Walt Whitman, Octavio Paz, Fairfield Porter, and Raymond Carver. You may view some of Marcus' photographs at www.flickr.com/photos/whynottryitagain2.

RICHARD WILE
ESTHER: A REMEMBRANCE
Creative Nonfiction

Richard Wile received his MFA in nonfiction from the University of Southern Maine's Stonecoast Creative Writing Program in 2005. His essays have been published in such diverse places as *Prairie Schooner*, *the Christian Century*, and *Cigar Aficionado*, as well as in an anthology, *Reflections on Maine*. He has recently completed a memoir, *Those That Mourn: A Memoir of Grief and Grace*. A native of Maine, he lives with his wife Mary Lee in an old family home in Yarmouth.

EDITOR BIOS

RELIEF'S EDITORS:

KIMBERLY CULBERTSON EDITOR-IN-CHIEF

Kimberly is a writer who found that the type of Christian writing that she was looking to read was difficult to find. She graduated from Bradley University and taught a few years in inner-city Chicago. In theory, she's working on a book about her time there, but in reality, she's pretty busy with this journal.

HEATHER VON DOEHREN ASSISTANT EDITOR

Heather received her bachelor's degree in English and secondary education with a minor in creative writing from Bradley University, home of Illinois Poet Laureate Kevin Stein. Currently, she is finishing her master's degree from the University of Arkansas.

BRAD FRUHAUFF POETRY EDITOR

Brad is a full-time student, part-time instructor, and sometime writer. While working on his Ph.D. in English, he is living in Evanston, IL, with his wife, Katie, and his two cats, to whom he discourses at length about the saints and sinners of contemporary Christian poetry, about the epistemological significance of syntax and punctuation, and of the existential and religious relevance of irony.

J. MARK BERTRAND FICTION EDITOR

In his time, Mark has been arrested for a crime he didn't commit, served as foreman of a hung jury, and gotten honorable mention in a modeling contest for children. He earned his MFA in Creative Writing at the University of Houston, where he was a production editor for the journal *Gulf Coast*. His recent fiction has appeared in *The New Pantagruel*, *Hardluck Stories*, and *The Ankeny Briefcase*. His nonfiction book, *Rethinking Worldview*, will be published by Crossway in October.

KAREN MIEDRICH-LUO CREATIVE NONFICTION EDITOR

Karen is a writer and language coach who lives in Plano, Texas. She has a BA in religion and philosophy from the University of Georgia and a post-graduate English Lit degree from the University of Houston. She was a staff writer for *Vision Magazine* 2002-2005. She also spent three years teaching English, writing, and history at Wuhan University in China where she met and married her husband, Brad. They have two daughters. She is currently writing a collection of essays about China and working on a book about her cross-cultural marriage. You can read her blog at www.miedrichluo.blogspot.com.

COACH CULBERTSON TECHNICAL EDITOR

Coach Culbertson, MCDBA, MCSA, MCT, is a Technical Instructor at New Horizons Computer Learning Center of Chicago, specializing in networking, database, and information management. He also consults on dynamic web technologies, graphic design, and ecommerce. In his spare time, he pretends to be a novelist and recently completed a fourth draft of his book *Coffee Shop Saints*. Since he is not nearly as cool as the other editors of *Relief*, he will probably complete a fifth, sixth, and seventh draft before he submits it to anyone. You can read his blog at www.coachculbertson.com or learn more about the Coffee Shop Saints at www.coffeeshopsaints.com.

the master's artist
many voices. a single purpose.

what is a master's artist?

The king gestures toward the tower window, indicating a vast kingdom spreading as far as the eye can see, and says, "Son, one day all of this will be yours."

The whiny, pathetic prince glances toward the window and says, "What? The curtains?"

Thus opens one of my favorite scenes from Monty Python and the Holy Grail. "Okay," you say. "That's dandy dialog for an absurd comedy. But why use it to open a post exploring what a Master's artist is?"

I'm so glad you asked.

a master's artist is...

small...

I love the final scene of Men in Black. The camera pans up from the street, out to the city, the nation, the world, the galaxy, to infinity and beyond, and the whole ball o' wax is contained in a single marble. What a great picture of how tiny we are! Of course, the good news is we're not being tossed around by aliens in some cosmic game. We're held in the palm of Almighty God, who transcends time and space and all created things. He can swirl galaxies in a celestial hoedown and still catch every silent tear shed in secret.

an heir...

Sometimes I think we're a lot like that wimpy prince. Our Father has given us great and glorious promises regarding our inheritance, but we can't see past the curtains. We set our hopes on things that are passing away—contracts, reputation, success, money—when God is gesturing at eternity and saying, "I have so much more for you."

a mirror...

Whether we like it or not, we are God's image to the world, and we have an obligation to keep ourselves unstained. Until we get sick of our narcissism, we won't be of much use to God. A mirror has no self-consciousness. It reflects whatever it faces. A Master's artist forsakes other loves (including fascination with her own gifts), and follows hard after God. She sets her face on Jesus.

We are artists because our Father is an artist. Creativity is our birthright. In and of ourselves we are no greater than the scu under God's fingernails, but He has humbled Himself and set His love upon us. And, as if that weren't enough, He's ushered into a broad place, tossed us the car keys, and said, "Go have fun, my obedient children. Find Me everywhere—even in Mon Python or Men in Black. Create something beautiful. Just remember, whatever you do is a reflection on Me."

Our King gestures toward the window and says, "All of this will someday be yours." Marvel, my fellow artists. He shares H inheritance with us, and we don't even deserve the curtains. —*Jeanne Damoff*

www.themastersartist.co

Introducing the
relief | writers network

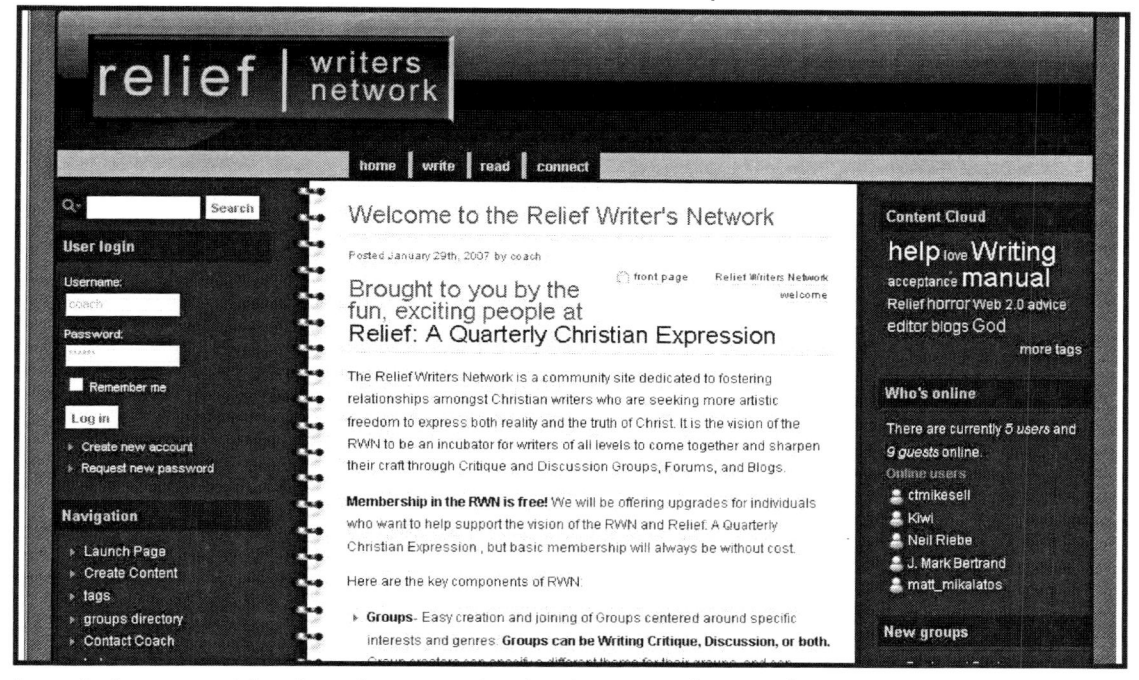

Introducing a new blog-based community site that not only provides an easy way to connect to other authors, readers, and editors, but also allows users to create their own communities for discussion, writing critique groups, and more. Take a look at some of the features of RWN:

—**Private Critique and Discussion Groups**—Every member can create their own critique or private discussion groups based on genre, type of writing, or whatever they like. Each group gets a private forum, event calendar, RSS feed, email notifications, and more! Groups will also have the capacity to publish their own eZine showcasing works by their members!

—**Work Upload**—In addition to posting your work directly on the site, you can upload your stories, poems, novels, etc, for other people to comment on.

—**AD FREE**—You will NEVER see banner ads, pop-ups, or any of the other annoying stuff you see on other sites.

—**Blog-O-Rama**—Everybody gets a blog to share thoughts, book reviews, etc.

—**Themes**—Don't like the way the site looks? Change it by using the Theme Switcher!

—**WYSIWYG Word Processor**—You can use a Word-like WYSIWYG (What You See Is What You Get) editor to easily format your posts.

—**Third-Party Integration**—PDF Generation, Technorati tagging, IM Online Status Indicators for Yahoo, AOL, Skype, Bible Gateway Instant Link Creation, and more.

—**All the standards**—Buddy lists, Private Messaging, Forums, Tag Clouds, Links, and more!

Get in on the ground floor of a community dedicated to a stronger sense of reality in Christian writing. Just go to www.reliefjournal.com and click on the Relief Writers Network button. We'll see you there!

The Ankeny Briefcase arrived Decemeber 1st. I know a lot of people said that hell would freeze over before it came out but it looks like they were wrong. Some people say it's the sign of the end of the world. Some people just say that they're glad it's coming out. Some people think it's a unigriff, the offspring of a hippgriff and unicorn. A lot of people might be angry after they read it. But that's okay. We think it's going to be neat. It's definitely not going to be your typical Guideposts devotional. Not to say that there's anything wrong with Guideposts. Guideposts is great. But Ankeny is just going to be different, that's all. As you can see, the Cardinal here is very staunch in his stance here. What is he so staunch about, anyway? Some stories in the Ankeny Briefcase will use words that some people don't like. But in real life some people use those words. Is it because they do not have a very large vocabulary? Maybe. Or maybe they grew up in a televisual age in which words have been stripped of their context and no longer mean what they used to mean. Maybe it's just elitism—some people think that people who swear are less than adequate, not suited for high society. Maybe they're right. Maybe we're missing information in our world today because advertisers think people are dumb and sell them stuff based on hype and not quality. Or maybe it's the opposite. I don't know. I wonder if the cardinal on this page knows why. He certainly looks like he does. The cardinal will be on the cover of the Ankeny Briefcase. Perhaps he will share his secret when it comes out. But probably not. He definitely looks like a proud cardinal. Maybe it's because he knows the secrets of the universe, and knows that if he tells anyone, they won't be secrets, and then he will have nothing to be proud about. But probably not. He is a very proud cardinal, after all, and he probably has many more things to be proud about, too. **You can purchase The Ankeny Briefcase for only fifteen bucks at <www.ankenybriefcase.com>.** It's quite a deal! And the cardinal will be on the cover with that proud but quirky smirk. Neat. Okey-doke. Good Bye Now. Time to go buy the book.

Christian Writing . . . Unbound

(Thank God)

Get **Relief** 4 times a year when you subscribe at www.reliefjournal.com. You save $19.76 when you subscribe, because Coach is so crazy, he's going to pay your shipping and handling for you and knock 95 cents off the cover price of each issue! Isn't that neat? We never know what he's going to do next, that crazy Coach.

So why wait? You've just read this issue and you know you liked it. Come on, now, don't lie. We know you did. So point that web browser right over to **www.reliefjournal.com/store** and subscribe today!

Coach's Midnight Diner will open its doors Summer 2007

Go to a comic book convention with Jesus and Chris Mikesell
Visit the nexus of the universe with Kevin Lucia
Evangelize at gunpoint with Charles Browning
Get into a street fight with Matt Mikalatos
Blow up some asteroids with Jens Rushing
Take swimming lessons with Nathan Knapp
Get De-mused with Mike Duran
Drink a little absinthe with Melody Graves
Go to a strip club with R.M. Oliver
Have a chat with Elvis and Jennifer Edwards
Find a little help with Linda Gilmore
Buy a whorehouse with Robert Garbacz
Take a trip to the moon with Neil Riebe
Catch the Night Train with Suzan Robertson
Give a gift to get a gift with Paul Luikart
Look into the eyes of a gargoyle with J. Mark Bertrand
Take the case with S.J. Kessel
Find the worm in the apple with Rob Jennings
Become a hero with Mike Dellosso
Go Old Testament on some bad guys with Mike Medina
Take a whole new look at statutory violence with Caroline Misner

Stay tuned to reliefjournal.com for details!

The following bonus piece, originally submitted to *Relief*, was one of many that inspired *Coach's Midnight Diner*. I'll be sneaking one story in at the end of every issue of *Relief*. "The Deluge" is an atypical spiritual warfare story, one in which the hero has a very unexpected but realistic reaction to something outside of his own point of view.

—Coach Culbertson
Editor, *Coach's Midnight Diner*

THE DELUGE
by Matt Mikalatos

Ted's mind cut a channel through the landscape of the world, running deep and strong and certain as a river. Camilla's mind moved much more like a weather system: unpredictable with flashes of great power, and in some way, which seemed very clear to Ted and nebulous to her, she generated his power, increased his depth and lessened his limitations.

Both of them were more like the crowds of *guan qian jie* than they would have ever thought. He moved in simple fashion up and down the great avenue, which he believed should not be called the "walking street" in all the tourist literature, because a street upon which no vehicle (not even the omnipresent bicycle) was allowed clearly could not be a street. His singular need—they were going to the ticket shop to buy train tickets for their trip tomorrow—dictated his direction, speed and patience. She, too, resembled the crowd with its diversity of focus, decisions being made more by intuition than conscious thought, the ebb and flow of thousands packed into a space for hundreds, some moving east, some west, some following an unseen, internal direction. The neon signs in Chinese—which he found garish—delighted her. Even the unintelligible Chinese pop music with its punctuated English ("*wo ai ni*, baby, wherever you are") she found charming and exotic. They reminded her of every reason she had left parents and friends and home and brought little Andy with them to China.

The one thing she could not bear on the half-mile stretch of the walking street was the temple, squat and silent as a spider at the center of *guan qian jie's* web of merchants. She shuddered and walked faster when need dictated that they pass it, as it did today. Ted could not understand this. But there had been other times when Camilla's nonsensical responses had proven correct, and so, in the year they had lived here, he had applied his great intellect to the temple to see if he could discover the root of her fears.

He had learned that it was not, as he had assumed, a Buddhist temple, but a Daoist one. After he learned this he noticed yin-yang symbols on the high wooden sides of it, and found he could see them most clearly when he took off his glasses and squinted. The temple had been built in honor of a general who had pleased an emperor a millennium ago and received a promotion from general to god. A wooden statue in his honor, fierce and brightly painted, loomed twelve feet higher than the small tables which sold sticks of incense and firecrackers wrapped in thin red paper. In all his observations—and he had made many, even coming to the temple without Camilla's knowledge to watch, to push against the walls of the temple with his mind—he had detected nothing insidious, frightening, or threatening. It seemed, in fact, nothing more than a cultural relic, a quaint reminder of a time when these streets and shops had been set aside to service a god, streets which now served capitalism and the needs of the people, now serviced those who needed train tickets and tennis shoes and tiny plastic animals to hang on the antennae of their mobile phones.

But the temple presented no danger to him, so he turned his attention to Camilla. She felt lonely, this seemed certain, for in their job they couldn't make friends with the other expatriates; other Americans picked up the cultural cues too readily and would surely make a slip, endangering Ted and Camilla's work. Americans came to China to make money, to make a getaway, or to make converts. This last purpose was illegal and Camilla and Ted were here to break that law. Perhaps the stress of this grated on Camilla in the same way that having the only white baby in the entire city ground them both down to dust. Even now, if they paused for the briefest moment, crowds of hundreds would form, crushing in to touch Andy's blond hair, to stroke him, to ask to hold him, to tell Camilla in Chinese that the baby was too hot, too cold, too skinny, and what white skin!

They were both encouraged by the work. Many people became Christians here and just this year their first church plant had split and grown into two more. But perhaps to her, the temple represented that the work would never be done, that they fought against thousands of years of tradition, and that if they were to see this job through to the end, then they must spend every last coin of their life here in the crowded marketplaces.

In the end he admitted that the temple's fearsome effect on his wife baffled him. She claimed to find a spiritual darkness there, a lingering, still-worshipped, malevolent spirit, the sort of thing that he knew existed but mostly stayed wedged firmly in the pages of the Gospels. Those things had passed, hadn't they, with the passing of so many other things, the speaking in tongues and prophecies and the voice of God speaking aloud in the temple while the rafters shook and smoke and darkness and lightning declared His presence. This temple, which crept up beside them even now with its shops prostrated before it, stemmed off of the walking street like a bulbous growth. The shops stood at a respectful distance, creating a spacious stone courtyard. Beautiful bridges that arched like spines crossed the stagnant canals and ushered one past the stone lion guardians. A waist-high, wrought-iron fence delineated a smaller courtyard within the greater one, and a strange black trough on high legs stood near the entrance, just behind the ticket booth. It cost a dollar to enter, and a short line of faithful worshippers shed their shoes on the way past the twelve-foot high double doors and into the thick shadows. Sticks of incense burned in sand-filled pedestals. The yellow walls gave it a cheery look, really, with the yin-yang symbols inserted high on the dark and jagged spires. It was an interesting building, yes, full of history, yes, but only a building nonetheless.

Somehow in the course of these thoughts Ted had let the squirming Andy out of his arms and Andy, newly captivated by the concept of running, slipped through the maze of legs and into the relatively open temple square. Camilla's sudden stiffness alerted Ted, brought him back to the immediate world. He called Andy's name and the boy giggled merrily. Ted shoved past a knot of college students and scooped him up. The college students pointed and laughed and took pictures with their phones. One of them asked if she could have a photo with Andy, but Ted pretended not to understand and moved away before they could get up the courage to try their English. As he stepped back into the crushing stream of shoppers he saw his wife, struggling forward through a crowd of admirers, and then, somehow, he noticed a man in a green sweater moving toward her with a singularity of purpose that startled him.

Camilla had taken to watching animal documentaries, because her Chinese was too primitive to understand even the children's shows on television. Animal documentaries seemed to explain themselves. Last week there had been one about sharks, and he had caught something about how a shark "locks on" to its prey, that if there were ninety seals it would choose one seal to follow, regardless of closer seals or even seals that got in the way. The man in the green sweater had that look, as if there were no one on the street other than Camilla; he fixed his eyes unwaveringly on her and moved through the crowd with a speed that Ted had not seen before. Ted sensed danger, but he was not a man who put much stock in senses that could not be clearly explained, and a man walking quickly over to see an American woman should not frighten him, though it did. He shook it off and called Camilla's name, his eyes fixed on the man.

The man's eyes snapped from Camilla to Ted and without missing a step he turned toward Ted and the writhing two-year-old in his arms. Ted wondered momentarily if the man could be with the government, or the local **PSB**, the police. Someone in their agency had been deported a week before from a nearby city. The man came closer and Ted realized that he was not coming straight at him, but seemed actually to be steering beyond him, toward the temple. Ted relaxed as the man passed on his left, and then, out of the corner of his eye he saw the man cock back his fist and take a vicious swing at his head. He saw it in time to turn his head away, and the fist caught him behind the ear, knocking his head into Andy's. Andy let out a cry of surprise and pain and Ted's first thought, rising to him unbidden and strange was, *In the name of Christ I command you to come out of him.*

This thought surprised him more than the punch, more than the throbbing, raised bruise already forming behind his ear, which his hand rose to touch and his fingers tentatively explored. He was not given to charismatic expressions, and in his church the devil had the good manners not to disturb the children of God. He could not put words to his unplanned thought, for he had no way of knowing if this man was truly demon-possessed. A misunderstanding seemed far more likely, and he quickly set Andy on the ground and told him to run to Mama. "Keep walking," he called to Camilla, who had cried out in horror and stood anchored now to the fitted stone street of *guan qian jie*. The crowd around her had already shifted toward him, to see what the foreigner would do after being punched in the head. "Keep walking," he repeated, and she did, but slowly, as if an anchor dragged behind her.

He tried to think of what to say to the man in the green sweater, who still stood beside him, a look of defiance on his face. "*Ni yao shenme?*" the man yelled, and Ted looked at him inquisitively, resettling the glasses on his face. One of the college students appeared at Ted's elbow and said quietly, "He is asking what do you want from him."

"But I don't want anything from him. Tell him I don't want anything."

The student looked down at the cobbled temple square. Camilla walked slowly toward the ticket seller, watching Ted the whole time. No one was in her way. "I do not wish to speak to him," the student said. "I cannot tell him your words. I am frightened. I am sorry."

Ted looked at the man in the green sweater, and his face was twisted with hate or sickness. He tried to say he wanted nothing, but the words came out wrong. "*Bu yao. Mei you.*"

The man in green snarled the words back, slurred and mocking, "*Bu yao mei you bu yao mei you. Ni yao shenme? NI YAO SHENME? NI WEISHENME JIAO WO?*"

"He says again what did you want with him and why did you call him."

"But I didn't call him. There's a misunderstanding."

The student, growing in boldness, spoke to the man. "*Ta mei you jiao ni.*" He didn't call you.

With an anguished cry the man swung his fist again, this time with such fierce savagery and speed that Ted did not see it until it was centimeters from his face. He had only time to close his eyes, and he felt his glasses break against his face, and then the bite of the cobbles beneath him. He opened his eyes in time to see a blurred shape in green moving away through the crowd, shouting obscenities and unintelligible, slurred Chinese.

Ted stood slowly. No one helped him. It would dishonor him and he would lose face. He fumbled with the two halves of his glasses and held them to his face to see the retreating figure more clearly. The man snapped at someone near him and then turned back toward Ted and snarled before moving on through the crowd.

Camilla called him. "Ted, are you okay?" He looked toward her. The crowd had moved toward his confrontation with the man in the green sweater as if pulled by gravity, and Camilla had been left beyond it, like the beach at low tide.

He dropped the broken glasses into his pocket and felt the knot behind his ear. His nose was bleeding, and he wiped it absently on his sleeve. He went to Camilla and Andy, who was crying. "I'm okay. Let's get our train tickets."

"That man. Did you know him?"

"No."

"We should tell the police."

The student still hovered at Ted's elbow, and he said, "There is a policeman there." He pointed ahead of them to a man in a dark blue uniform, a whistle around his neck. His job was to blow his whistle at people who brought their bicycles onto the walking street. Ted walked over toward him without thought, drawn to his symbols of power and the authority he represented. Surely he could make this right.

Ted went to him and got his attention. "A man hit me," he said in his simple Chinese. "He wore a green sweater. He . . . he hit me in the face."

The police officer looked to the student and they burst into a rapid-fire conversation, only a few words of which Ted understood. An old woman had followed them from the temple square and she gave Andy a candy, which stopped his crying. The student and the officer grew more animated until at last the student pointed the way the man in the green sweater had gone. The old lady interjected something here, and then both the officer and the student dropped their heads and nodded. The officer called something in on his walkie-talkie but then he turned away from Ted.

"What's happening," Camilla said. "What's he doing?"

"I don't know. I guess calling in that guy, telling the other police where he's headed."

"No," said the student. "I am sorry. There is nothing he can do. The man is crazy."

"So they should go and arrest him, get him off the street."

The student shook his head. "He is crazy. His head is bad. There is nothing he can do."

Ted pulled on the sleeve of the officer to get his attention and the officer pulled it forcefully away and pointedly did not look at Ted. "I am sorry," the student said again. "You are a good man not to hit him after he hit you. His head is very bad and we all are sad for him. We all are afraid of him." With that the student turned and walked into the crowd and the old lady with him. Ted and Camilla and Andy stood alone in a wash of faces that looked all the same, every one of them identical to the man who had punched him.

Ted held Camilla. She had Andy in her arms, still sucking on his candy and content. Ted let Camilla go and said, "Why don't you two walk home and I'll go get the train tickets. I don't want you to stay here after that."

"I'm not walking home alone," Camilla said. "What if that man sees me and Andy? Or what if he comes back here to find you?"

"He won't come back," Ted said. "That wouldn't make any sense. Why come back here now?"

Camilla's eyes flicked to the temple and back again to Ted. "He's insane, Ted. Didn't they say that? Doesn't that mean that he often does things that make no sense? He could be watching us right now, Ted. He could have a knife." She shuddered. "Let's get the tickets and go home."

They bought the tickets. The crowds kept flowing as before, though people noticed his nose and he heard the word for blood whispered all around them. As they walked home he kept increasing their pace. He was nervous. He looked into the crowd for that green sweater over and over but did not see it. Could the man have been possessed? It seemed ludicrous. And if it were true, if he were possessed, then it pounded open everything Ted believed about the universe, it made a terrifying and dark space spread out before him like a cavern.

"Everyone in this town knows where we live," Camilla said. "We're the only white family in three miles. That man could find us without trying. We have to lock the doors tonight. I want Andy to sleep where I can hear him."

Ted said nothing because Camilla was absolutely right. They left the walking street at last and then the final six blocks to their apartment, past the guard who fell asleep every night promptly at eleven, through the locked gates to the cement stairway. As he turned the bolt to their apartment door he felt profoundly vulnerable, naked, afraid. He locked all the doors and windows in the house, even the glass door which only looked down on the shared courtyard. During dinner he kept standing up and walking into the bedroom, holding his glasses to his face and looking down on the street, trying to see if a man with a green sweater might be standing there looking up into their apartment.

They put Andy to bed but worried about leaving him alone in the room even though they were on the third floor. They moved his crib into their bedroom, which seemed somehow safer even though they were still sitting in the living room. After a long time Ted told her about the flash of a thought that he should exorcise the man who had punched him. He expected her to laugh at him, or to mock him. Instead she shrugged and said, "If it was God speaking to you, you should have done it. If it wasn't him, well, it wouldn't have done you any harm to try it." She believed in that, that God could speak in a moment, in a flash of insight. He had never experienced this, or if he had, he had not trusted it. God had the Bible, and this clear and precise set of rules and guidelines seemed the work of a deity to Ted, unlike the mess of communicating to the disordered mind of a human creature.

He couldn't sleep. He stared for many hours at the cement ceiling, watching the shifting pools of yellow light from the street lamps. He listened carefully for Andy's breathing. Camilla curled up close to him, much closer than she usually slept. He listened, too, for any change in the traffic pattern, any disturbance, any ripple of abnormality. He wondered eventually if he would really hear anything if the man in the green sweater came near his window, and soon he found himself standing beneath the window's floor-length curtain, his forehead pressed to the cold glass. He couldn't keep his glasses together for long and he set them down on the cement sill. Blue taxis and the occasional bicycle slipped past. A few drunks held each other up as they left the neon-lighted bars. He could see the temple in the distance, lit by the markets and restaurants, squatted down and holding court with its acolytes.

He stood for a long time debating the sentence he would speak. He debated getting his Bible, but in the end he knew what it said, knew what it would tell him. "In the name of Christ," he whispered, "I command you to come out of him." He stared at the temple, waiting for some response and when there was none he said it louder, "Come out!" It had begun to rain, and bicyclists whipped by, pulling on their rain ponchos, a parade of blue, yellow and red plastic sheets spinning beneath him. His fingers fumbled at the window lock and he feverishly slid it open. The rain increased, and the wind blew against him. "In Christ's name!" He was shouting now. "Come out of him now!" The rain broke the sky at last and great opaque sheets of it descended on the city and beat against his face and chest. He listened attentively to the sound of the rain hitting the gutters, flooding the broken green tiles of the sidewalk. He intently directed his attention to the distant temple, demanding that the spirits obey, but he could not keep up the intense focus for long.

    He slid down to the floor, spent. He reached behind himself and slid the window awkwardly closed and lay there for a moment on the floor, wet, cold, exhausted. He used the windowsill to pull himself to his knees. Nothing he could see had changed. The temple, the markets, the bars, the bicyclists and taxis, all sat and sold and spun through the rain. After toweling himself dry and checking on Andy he lay back in bed where his wife kindly did not speak, but put her head again on his chest and her arm across it. At the edge of sleep at last he heard a great, tortured shriek from deep in the city's labyrinth. Whether from the brakes of a passing bus or something else he could not say.

    The sun, when it came, at last dispelled all shreds of darkness, all hints of rain, all scraps of cloud and made the cement shimmer. Ted stretched his arms and enjoyed the sunlight blanketing his wife and son. Let them sleep! He explored the altered topography of his face in the mirror of the closet-sized bathroom. His nose belonged on a larger man, and he painfully removed some clotted blood. By folding his left ear back he could see the grey and green signs of a man's fist. He moved into the living room and sat on the orange sherbet-colored vinyl couch which the apartment complex had provided. He was glad his family slept, because he needed time to catalogue the events of the last twenty-four hours.

    The entire landscape of Ted's world had altered, and all of his maps were suddenly changed. The man in green had thrown boulders into the river of his mind and had disrupted the flow, had created rapids, had troubled the waters. Beyond that, however, and more disturbing still, was another feeling, something Ted did not recognize and could not explain. A feeling that a great wall of water was coming from upstream, that a dam had broken somewhere and all that Ted knew, all the man in green had done, everything would be swallowed up and buried beneath it.

    Ted pulled the curtains open and looked down on the courtyard. The sunlight changed everything. He felt ridiculous now for shouting out his bedroom window in the middle of the night, for letting the rain pummel him. He had behaved in a superstitious way, as if shouting a few words out his window would have influence in the world. It was a shamanistic and ignorant worldview. He laughed, relieved. He went to Andy's bedroom and opened the curtains there, too. He looked down at the new morning traffic, the bikes and taxis on their way to work, the bus with the loudspeaker rounding the corner and projecting garbled Chinese.

Ted suddenly desired to return to the temple square. Another look at the temple in the daylight would dispel the last of his doubts, he was certain of it. And if he saw the man in the green sweater again, well, what of it? He checked in on Camilla and Andy again, to make sure they were still sleeping. A thought struck him and he took the three salmon-colored train tickets from his wallet. It seemed to him that the train was too early now, that his family should be allowed to sleep. He would run down to the ticket seller and buy new, later tickets. This gave him a good reason to pass the temple, a readily explainable one, a logical one. He could slip out to the temple and be back before they woke. He pulled on clothes and a jacket and then, by the door, his shoes.

Saturday morning meant that the walking street would be a standing street within an hour or so. He hurried past the neon signs, the eight-foot tall trees in their big wooden pots and the pop-blaring shoe stores. He held his breath as the temple came into view, worried that the sunshine wouldn't work its magic on the multi-hued wood. He quickly scanned the crowd and did not see the man in the green sweater. Ted hoped the man would still be wearing the green sweater, the badge of his identity. If he came, Ted would see him first. Ted forced himself to be calm. He stopped and bought two wooden skewers of lamb's meat. They were cooked over charcoals right across from the temple square, and dusted with ground red pepper. It was an ordinary day. He had walked into the temple square a hundred times before, and he would do so again today.

He began in the small shop at the temple square's entrance and looked over the incense sticks and firecrackers, the little postcards, the shallow dish of cash offerings. Nothing had changed here. He stepped past the guardian lions, crossing the arched bridge. Surely if malevolent spirits guarded this place the lions would have roared! He smiled and took a bite of lamb, beginning to enjoy himself. He took a deep breath and sat on a stone bench. He looked fondly at the quaint yellow temple. He had thought the sunlight would make it harmless, but he saw now that it was the power of his own intellect that did it, for the sun had gone behind a cloud and the dropping temperature told him it would rain soon.

Ted stood to go buy the new train tickets and to throw away the empty wooden skewers in his hand and as he did he heard a shout from across the temple square. He looked up and saw the man in the green sweater coming toward him from around the side of the temple, coming toward him fast. Ted turned and moved toward the bridge, determined to move quickly away from the man. Then he saw the second man, pushing people out of his way and headed toward Ted. He wore tan slacks, a gray-checked shirt and a rumpled tan jacket over it. The second man called something to the man in the green sweater. Ted did not understand it all, but he heard the word for foreigner.

For a moment he froze, uncertain where to go. The man in the tan jacket blocked the bridge, and the man in the green sweater would cut him off if he went the other way. His heart pounded in his ears, and the blood rushing to his head throbbed through his swollen face and bruised head. He decided to take his chances with the new man rather than the man in green, so he ran toward the bridge. He tried to barrel past the new man, but he grabbed Ted by the shirt collar and yanked him back, hard.

Without thinking Ted jabbed one of the wooden skewers into the man's shoulder, and it splintered to pieces as the man fell backward. Ted couldn't stop. He kept running, crossing the bridge and then diving into the crowd of shoppers. He turned to the right and began to push past the slow-moving old men and women, the college students holding hands, the tourists following the guide with the yellow flag. Just up ahead was where the policeman had stood yesterday, and Ted knew if he could get to him he would be safe. He hoped the man in the green sweater would pause to help his friend, but he thought again of the shark, the unrelenting hunter. Ted knocked into a man carrying a baby, but he couldn't stop even to apologize, he had to keep going.

The policeman stood at the side of the street, yelling at a man who had tried to bring his bicycle onto the walking street. Ted grabbed hold of him and yanked him away from the conversation. He gasped for air. "*Yo yiga ren,*" he said. "*Ta yao da wo.*" He turned back and pointed to his pursuer. But he was not there. The policeman unclasped Ted's hands from his shirt and pulled away. He studied Ted for a moment. Ted could see the look of recognition. A veil descended over the officer's face and he turned back to the bicyclist. The officer waved him off without looking at him again.

Precious seconds had been wasted on the policeman, and Ted knew he stood out in the crowd. He was afraid to go back past the temple toward his house, and afraid to stay in the street where he stood out in the sea of Chinese people. The man in green and his friend came skidding across the arched bridge of the temple courtyard, scanning the crowd around them. Ted ducked into a department store, jumping over the two stairs at the entrance and pushing in past the disgusting plastic flaps that hung in the doorway. He walked quickly past a few rows of shoes and tried to catch his breath, tried to calm his heart. He felt for his mobile phone in the pocket of his jacket, and held it in his hand. He could call the police, but his Chinese wasn't good enough to explain anything. He could call Camilla but it would only terrify her. She couldn't call the police, either, couldn't do anything but worry. And she might come down here and put Andy and herself in danger.

He crouched down behind the shoe rack, pretending to look at a pair of loafers but actually looking out through the front entrance. He knew there was another entrance behind him somewhere, probably on the far corner of the building. He saw a flash of green run past outside, running too fast for Ted's liking. But then, even worse, the green blur came back, lingered outside the department store. Ted could see the man trying to look in through the plastic flaps, debating if it was worth the time to stick his head inside or to keep running. Then he moved slowly on, and Ted breathed again.

If he waited a few minutes and slipped back toward home he might have a chance. He hoped the man in green didn't know where he lived, but everyone in the city knew where the white family lived, so this seemed unlikely. He hoped the man didn't think to wait for him somewhere between here and his apartment.

Ted turned and quickly scanned the department store behind him in time to see the second man, the one he had stabbed, coming in through the far door. Ted crouched low, but it didn't help. Shoppers started to gather around him, anxious to see the foreigner's strange shoe-shopping ritual. He tried to wave them away, but it didn't work and when he turned again to look the man was moving warily toward him. Ted looked in his hands. He had dropped the other skewer somewhere. He only held his mobile phone now.

As if having the same thought, the man took out his own mobile phone, punched a number in and held it to his ear, never taking his eyes off of Ted. Ted glanced frantically at the door, then back to the man. He was talking now, and slowly moving forward, keeping himself between Ted and the far door. Ted stepped out from between the shoes and backed away. The man said something to him now, something about being friends, but Ted could not understand, all of the Chinese in his brain had been shut off and replaced with survival. He turned and sprinted through the door and smashed directly into the man in green, sending him sprawling down the two stairs and onto the paving stones. Ted half fell, kept moving forward, got his feet under him and ran, back toward home. He had a long way to go still, but he found the crowd working to his advantage. People were shouting and looking back at him, clumping up as he passed. The crowd slowed Ted's pursuers. He was losing them.

The rain started then, a sudden shower. The crowd was gone as suddenly as the rain had come, standing underneath the eaves of the buildings, holding newspapers over their heads, the women shrieking, the men calmly and methodically moving them to dry overhangs, into shops. Ted ran faster, but the wet stones of the street were slick and he nearly lost his footing. The man in green shouted something again, and Ted looked back at him. The desperate look on the man's face did nothing to comfort Ted, and neither did the fact that now, just now, he was passing the temple square. The rain poured furiously and pooled up in the center drains on the streets. Ted's feet kicked up waves as he ran toward his apartment. The man in green was gaining—Ted could hear his pursuer's footsteps over the pounding of the rain. He lost his footing, slid a few feet, windmilled his arms and slammed into the ground. He flew forward through a puddle, his entire body wet and his mobile phone smashing to pieces as it hit the ground. The man in green tripped over Ted's body, flew beyond him and hit the cobbles, hard, with his face.

Ted struggled to his feet, but the man in green stayed on the ground, on his knees in a puddle. Ted stepped past the man in green, trying to stay out of reach, but the man grabbed hold of Ted's leg. Ted pulled away, panting, aching. He couldn't run anymore. Something in his leg burned, and it felt like his hip had popped out of joint. He could hardly stand.

The man in green tried to stand and Ted punched him in the face as hard as he could, knocking him to the ground. When the man tried to stand again Ted punched him again, catching him under the eye and knocking him back to the ground. He followed it with a kick that landed somewhere between stomach and shoulder. The man in green spit blood into the street and then crawled toward Ted. "What do you want from me?" Ted yelled. He pushed his soaked hair from his face. "What do you want?" He stepped backward, away from the wretched man.

The man in green looked to the rain-drenched temple, as if weighing it. He turned his face back up to Ted and held his palms out toward him and rattled off a sentence that Ted could not follow, but it was not the slurred rant of the day before. "*Shuo yi bian,*" Ted said. "Say it again."

The man began to sob, his shoulders shaking. He put his hands flat on the pavement and an anguished cry echoed off the walls of the shops, the temple, the restaurants.

The man in the green sweater did not look up from the ground when he spoke. "*Duibuqi,*" he said, choking on his own voice. "*Wo bu yao da ni. Duibuqi.*" I'm sorry. I didn't want to hit you.

Ted stood there, letting the rain use him like a drum. He did not know what to do. He did not know where to put his hands. He could not move, could not think. His hip hurt. His face burned where it had skid along the stone. His entire hand ached, though his knuckles hurt the worst and seemed to be swelling already.

The man looked back up to Ted, his lips drawn back and showing his teeth, mucous and tears and saliva and blood all running from the man's face and gathering in the rainwater below him. The man tried to draw breaths but only deep wheezing sobs would come. Ted kneeled down beside him in the rain. The man could not even look at him. Ted cautiously took hold of the man's forearms and told him through his hands that it didn't matter, that he forgave him. The man shook his head violently, the tears unstoppable. He looked again at the temple and shook his head as if clearing a troubling thought or a bad dream. He looked up to Ted, locked eyes with him, his hands tightening on Ted's sleeves. His sobs subsided to short jerks of breath.

"*Wo nüer bingle*," he said, and the great effort of saying those words told Ted that the man was confiding something in him, was asking something from him. He searched the man's face for a clue, some sign of how to respond, but all he saw was the bruise forming beneath his eye where Ted had punched him, and a knot on his forehead where it had hit the paving stones.

"I don't understand," Ted said. "Your daughter is sick? What do you want me to do? *Ni yao shenme?*"

And the next words took Ted a moment to translate in his head. He looked to the puddle of water between them while he searched for the meaning of the words, and when he found it he looked back to the man in confusion, for he had said, "Please come to my house, and pray for her."

Ted tried to formulate an answer. He stared at the cobbled street and the stream of water rushing past him to the drains. He opened his mouth to speak and closed it again. He looked up again to the man, and the man stood and gathered the pieces of Ted's mobile phone. He placed them in Ted's hands. Ted could not see a way to repair it. A chunk of the casing was gone, the screen was cracked, the antenna snapped in half. The man stood ten feet behind him now, gesturing toward another street and calling to him. Ted wondered if he should stand and follow him. He wondered if he could just go home, and what Camilla would say.

Another minute passed and the man's shoulders fell. He turned and began to walk away, looking at Ted one last time, imploringly. Then the rain lightened and at last stopped, and a flood of people washed around him. For a brief moment Ted could see the man's green sweater in that tide, sweeping through the new and golden sunlight. Then the man in the green sweater was gone, replaced with a thousand like him, all streaming toward the market, or the temple, or distant, unseen destinations. Ted stood unmoving for a moment, searching for one last glimpse of green. Then the crowd swept him toward home, the temple at his back and receding. He turned back once to see it, but the sun flooded everything and he saw only a brilliant and unutterable whiteness beyond the bridge, a construction of light and moisture, as if a mighty hand had reached down and spread a curtain over the temple, as if the ground had swallowed it.

He would hold Andy when he got home and not think of the sick girl or her father at all, not for hours afterwards; he would only think on this edifice of light. He would reflect on the peculiar way the light washed the temple from the sky. Ted touched his hip and limped toward home, eager to see Camilla's face in the window, eager to lift his hand in greeting and show her that he was safe, and that they were beyond all harm.

MATT MIKALATOS knew the dame was trouble. She pointed a pistol at him.

"I have a job for you," she said. "At the Diner."

He pulled her to him, rough. "That place ain't safe, sister. That's why I live in Washington. I got a wife and two daughters to protect." He could take a punch, sure, but the Diner was full of crooks, chthonic entities, zombies.

He snatched the gun from her. He would take the job. He always did. He brushed past her and headed down the fog-bound street toward Coach's Midnight Diner. He would need the pistol before sunrise.